EX LIBRIS

VINTAGE CLASSICS

THE SNOW GHOST
AND
OTHER TALES

Classic Japanese Ghost Stories

VINTAGE CLASSICS

3 5 7 9 10 8 6 4

Vintage Classics is part of the Penguin Random House
group of companies whose addresses can be found
at global.penguinrandomhouse.com

This edition published in 2024
First published by Vintage Classics in 2023

penguin.co.uk/vintage-classics

Typeset in 11.4/14pt Bembo Book MT Pro by Jouve (UK), Milton Keynes
Printed and bound in Great Britain by Clays Ltd, Elcograf S.p.A.

The authorised representative in the EEA is Penguin Random House Ireland,
Morrison Chambers, 32 Nassau Street, Dublin D02 YH68

A CIP catalogue record for this book is available from the British Library

ISBN 9781784878733

Contents

A Note on the Text

The stories in this collection are sourced from a variety of books by Lafcadio Hearn, Yei Theodora Ozaki and Richard Gordon Smith, all dating from around the turn of the twentieth century. Those books are Lafcadio Hearn's *Kokoro* (1895), *In Ghostly Japan* (1899), *Kottō* (1902), *Kwaidan* (1904) and *Kimiko* (1923), Yei Theodora Ozaki's *Japanese Fairy Tales* (1903) and Richard Gordon Smith's *Ancient Tales and Folklore of Japan* (1908). These works were composed during a time of great transition in Japan as it grappled with modernising forces, as well as a period of deep fascination with traditional Japanese culture in the West.

All the stories collected here were originally written in English for the purpose of introducing a Western readership to the folklore and mythology of Japanese culture, and as such originally included footnotes and references to aid the reader's understanding. For this edition, we have retained as few footnotes from the original texts as possible, taking the liberty to abridge those we have kept so they remain unobtrusive yet provide context where necessary. Where some footnotes originally provided a simple translation, we have included that in the text in brackets. Otherwise, the stories remain unaltered. Finally, we have added initials and the year of publication at the end of each story to indicate the author and collection from which these tales were sourced.

The Snow Ghost and Other Tales

The Goblin of Adachigahara

Long, long ago there was a large plain called Adachigahara, in the Province of Mutsu in Japan. This place was said to be haunted by a cannibal goblin who took the form of an old woman. From time to time many travellers disappeared and were never heard of more, and the old women around the charcoal braziers in the evenings, and the girls washing the household rice at the wells in the mornings, whispered dreadful stories of how the missing folk had been lured to the goblin's cottage and devoured, for the goblin lived only on human flesh. No one dared to venture near the haunted spot after sunset, and all those who could, avoided it in the daytime, and travellers were warned of the dreaded place.

One day as the sun was setting, a priest came to the plain. He was a belated traveller, and his robe showed that he was a Buddhist pilgrim walking from shrine to shrine to pray for some blessing or to crave forgiveness of sins. He had apparently lost his way, and as it was late he met no one who could show him the road or warn him of the haunted spot.

He had walked the whole day and was now tired and hungry, and the evenings were chilly, for it was late autumn, and he began to be very anxious to find some house where he could obtain a night's lodging. He found himself lost in the midst of the large plain, and looked about in vain for some sign of human habitation.

At last, after wandering about for some hours, he saw a clump of trees in the distance, and through the trees he caught sight of the glimmer of a single ray of light. He exclaimed with joy:

'Oh, surely that is some cottage where I can get a night's lodging!'

Keeping the light before his eyes, he dragged his weary, aching feet as quickly as he could towards the spot, and soon came to a miserable-looking little cottage. As he drew near he saw that it was in a tumbledown condition, the bamboo fence was broken and weeds and grass pushed their way through the gaps. The paper screens which serve as windows and doors in Japan were full of holes, and the posts of the house were bent with age and seemed scarcely able to support the old thatched roof. The hut was open, and by the light of an old lantern an old woman sat industriously spinning.

The pilgrim called to her across the bamboo fence and said:

'O *Baa San* (Old Woman), good evening! I am a traveller! Please excuse me, but I have lost my way and do not know what to do, for I have nowhere to rest tonight. I beg you to be good enough to let me spend the night under your roof.'

The old woman, as soon as she heard herself spoken to, stopped spinning, rose from her seat and approached the intruder.

'I am very sorry for you. You must indeed be distressed to have lost your way in such a lonely spot so late at night. Unfortunately, I cannot put you up, for I have no bed to offer you, and no accommodation whatsoever for a guest in this poor place!'

'Oh, that does not matter,' said the priest. 'All I want is a shelter under some roof for the night, and if you will be good enough just to let me lie on the kitchen floor I shall be grateful.

I am too tired to walk further tonight, so I hope you will not refuse me, otherwise I shall have to sleep out on the cold plain.' And in this way he pressed the old woman to let him stay.

She seemed very reluctant, but at last she said:

'Very well, I will let you stay here. I can offer you a very poor welcome only, but come in now and I will make a fire, for the night is cold.'

The pilgrim was only too glad to do as he was told. He took off his sandals and entered the hut. The old woman then brought some sticks of wood and lit the fire, and bade her guest draw near and warm himself.

'You must be hungry after your long tramp,' said the old woman. 'I will go and cook some supper for you.' She then went to the kitchen to cook some rice.

After the priest had finished his supper, the old woman sat down by the fireplace and they talked together for a long time. The pilgrim thought to himself that he had been very lucky to come across such a kind, hospitable old woman. At last the wood gave out, and as the fire died slowly down he began to shiver with cold just as he had done when he arrived.

'I see you are cold,' said the old woman. 'I will go out and gather some wood, for we have used it all. You must stay and take care of the house while I am gone.'

'No, no,' said the pilgrim, 'let me go instead, for you are old and I cannot think of letting you go out to get wood for me this cold night!'

The old woman shook her head and said:

'You must stay quietly here, for you are my guest.' Then she left him and went out.

In a minute she came back and said:

'You must sit where you are and not move, and whatever happens, don't go near or look into the inner room. Now mind what I tell you!'

'If you tell me not to go near the back room, of course I won't,' said the priest, rather bewildered.

The old woman then went out again and the priest was left alone. The fire had died out and the only light in the hut was that of a dim lantern. For the first time that night he began to feel that he was in a weird place, and the old woman's words, 'Whatever you do, don't peep into the back room,' aroused his curiosity and his fear.

What hidden thing could be in that room that she did not wish him to see? For some time the remembrance of his promise to the old woman kept him still, but at last he could no longer resist his curiosity to peep into the forbidden place.

He got up and began to move slowly towards the back room. Then the thought that the old woman would be very angry with him if he disobeyed her made him come back to his place by the fireside.

As the minutes went slowly by and the old woman did not return, he began to feel more and more frightened, and to wonder what dreadful secret was in the room behind him. He must find out.

'She will not know that I have looked unless I tell her. I will just have a peep before she comes back,' said the man to himself.

With these words he got up on his feet (for he had been sitting all this time in Japanese fashion with his feet under him) and stealthily crept towards the forbidden spot. With trembling hands he pushed back the sliding door and looked in. What he saw froze the blood in his veins. The room was full of dead men's bones and the walls were splashed and the floor was covered with human blood. In one corner, skull upon skull rose to the ceiling, in another was a heap of arm bones, in another a heap of leg bones. The sickening smell made him faint. He fell backwards with horror and for some time lay in a heap with fright on the floor, a pitiful sight. He trembled all over and his teeth chattered, and he could hardly crawl away from the dreadful spot.

'How horrible!' he cried out. 'What awful den have I come to in my travels? May Buddha help me or I am lost. Is it possible that that kind old woman is really the cannibal goblin? When she comes back she will show herself in her true character and eat me up at one mouthful!'

With these words his strength came back to him and, snatching up his hat and staff, he rushed out of the house as fast as his legs could carry him. Out into the night he ran, his one thought to get as far as he could from the goblin's haunt. He had not gone far when he heard steps behind him and a voice crying, 'Stop! Stop!'

He ran on, redoubling his speed, pretending not to hear. As he ran, he heard the steps behind him come nearer and nearer, and at last he recognised the old woman's voice, which grew louder and louder as she came nearer.

'Stop! Stop, you wicked man! Why did you look into the forbidden room?'

The priest quite forgot how tired he was and his feet flew over the ground faster than ever. Fear gave him strength, for he knew that if the goblin caught him he would soon be one of her victims. With all his heart he repeated the prayer to Buddha:

'*Namu Amida Butsu, Namu Amida Butsu.*'

And after him rushed the dreadful old hag, her hair flying in the wind and her face changing with rage into the demon that she was. In her hand she carried a large blood-stained knife, and she still shrieked after him, 'Stop! Stop!'

At last, when the priest felt he could run no more, the dawn broke, and with the darkness of night the goblin vanished and he was safe. The priest now knew that he had met the Goblin of Adachigahara, the story of whom he had often heard, but never believed to be true. He felt that he owed his wonderful escape to the protection of Buddha to whom he had prayed for help, so he took out his rosary and, bowing his head as the sun rose, he said his prayers and made his thanksgiving earnestly. He then set forward for another part of the country, only too glad to leave the haunted plain behind him.

Y. T. O.
1903

White Bone Mountain

At the foot of Mount Shumongatake, up in the north-western Province of Echigo, once stood – and probably even still stands in rotten or repaired state – a temple of some importance, inasmuch as it was the burial ground of the feudal Lord Yamana's ancestors. The name of the temple was Fumonji, and many high and important priests kept it up, generation after generation, owing to the early help received from Lord Yamana's relations. Among the priests who presided over this temple was one named Ajari Joan, who was the adopted son of the Otomo family.

Ajari was learned and virtuous, and had many followers; but one day the sight of a most attractive girl called Kiku (Chrysanthemum), whose age was eighteen, upset all his religious equilibrium. He fell desperately in love with her, offering to sacrifice his position and reputation if she would only listen to his prayer and marry him; but the lovely O-Kiku San refused all his entreaties. A year later, she was taken seriously ill with fever and died, and whispers went abroad that Ajari the priest had cursed her in his jealousy and brought about her illness and her death. The rumour was not exactly without reason, for Ajari went mad within a week of O-Kiku's death. He neglected his services and then got worse, running wildly about the temple, shrieking at night and frightening all those who came near.

Finally, one night he dug up the body of O-Kiku and ate part of her flesh.

People declared that he had turned into the Devil, and none dared go near the temple; even the younger priests left, until at last he was alone. So terrified were the people, none approached the temple, which soon ran to rack and ruin. Thorny bushes grew on the roof, moss on the hitherto polished and matted floors; birds built their nests inside, perched on the mortuary tablets, and made a mess of everything; the temple, which had once been a masterpiece of beauty, became a rotting ruin.

One summer evening, some six or seven months later, an old woman who owned a teahouse at the foot of Shumongatake Mountain was about to close her shutters when she was terrified at the sight of a priest with a white cap on his head approaching.

'The Devil Priest! The Devil Priest!' she cried as she slammed the last shutter in his face. 'Get away, get away! We can't have you here.'

'What do you mean by "Devil Priest"? I am a travelling or pilgrim priest, not a robber. Let me in at once, for I want both rest and refreshment,' cried the voice from outside.

The old woman looked through a crack in the shutters and saw that it was not the dreaded maniac, but a venerable pilgrim priest: so she opened the door and let him in, profuse in her apologies, and telling him how they were all frightened out of their wits by the priest of Fumonji Temple, who had gone mad over a love affair.

'Oh, sir, it is truly terrible! We hardly dare go within half a mile of the temple now, and some day the mad priest is sure to come out of it and kill some of us.'

'Do you mean to tell me that a priest has so far forgotten himself as to break through the teachings of Buddha and make himself the slave of worldly passions?' asked the traveller.

'I don't know about the worldly passions,' cried the old lady, 'but our priest has turned into a devil, as all the people here-abouts will tell you, for he has even dug up and eaten of the flesh of the poor girl whom he caused to die by his cursing!'

'There have been instances of people turning devils,' said the priest, 'but they are usually common people and not priests. A courtier of the Emperor So's turned into a serpent; the wife of Yosei into a moth; the mother of Ogan into a *Yasha* (vampire bat), but I have never heard of a priest turning into a devil. Besides, Ajari Joan, your priest at Fumonji Temple, was a virtu-ous and clever man, I have always heard. I have come here, in fact, to do myself the honour of meeting him, and tomorrow I shall go and see him.'

The old lady served the priest with tea and begged him to think of no such thing, but he persisted and said that on the morrow he would do as he mentioned, and read the mad priest a lecture; and then he laid himself down to rest for the night.

Next afternoon the old priest, true to his word, started for the Fumonji Temple, the old lady accompanying him for the first part of the walk, to the place where the path which led to the temple turned up the mountain, and there she bade him goodbye, refusing to go another step.

The sun was beginning to set as the priest came in sight of the temple, and he saw that the place was in great disorder. The gates had tumbled off their hinges, withered leaves were thickly strewn everywhere and crumpled under his feet; but he walked boldly on, and struck a small temple bell with his staff. At the sound came many birds and bats from the temple, the bats flap-ping around his head; but there was no other sign of life. He struck the bell again with renewed force, and it boomed and clanged in echoes. At last a thin, miserable-looking priest came out, and, looking wildly about, said:

'Who are you, and why have you come here? The temple has

long since been deserted, for some reason which I cannot understand. If you want lodging you must go to the village. There is neither food nor bedding here.'

'I am a priest from Wakasa Province. The pretty scenery and clear streams have caused me to linger long on my journey. It is too late now to go to the village and I am too tired: so please let me remain for the night,' said the priest. The other made answer:

'I cannot order you away. This place is no longer more than a ruined shed. You can stay if you like, but you can have neither food nor bedding.' Having said this, he sat on the corner of a rock, while the pilgrim priest sat on another, close by. Neither spoke until it was dark and the moon had risen. Then the mad priest said, 'Find what place you can inside to sleep. There are no beds, but what there is of the roof keeps the mountain dew from falling on you during the night, and it falls heavily here and wets you through.' Then he went into the temple – the pilgrim priest could not tell where, for it was dark and he could not follow, the place being littered with idols and beams and furniture, which the mad priest had hacked to pieces in the early stages of his madness. The pilgrim, therefore, felt his way about until he found himself between a large fallen idol and a wall; and here he decided to spend the night, it being as safe a place in which to hide from the maniac as any he could find without knowing his way about or having a light. Fortunately for himself, he was a strong and healthy old man and was well able to do without food, and also to stand, unharmed, the piercing and damp cold. The pilgrim priest could hear the sound of the many streams which gurgled down the mountainside. There was also the unpleasant sound of squeaking rats as they chased and fought, and of bats which flew in and out of the place, and of hooting owls; but beyond this, nothing – nothing of the mad priest. Hour after hour passed thus until one o'clock, when suddenly, just as the pilgrim felt himself dozing off, he was aroused by a noise. The whole temple seemed as if it were being knocked down. Shutters were slammed with such violence that they fell to the floor; right and left, idols and furniture were being hurled about. In and out ran the sound of the naked, pattering feet of the crazed priest, who shouted:

'Oh, where is the beautiful O-Kiku, my sweetly beloved Kiku? Oh, where, oh, where is she? The gods and the devils have combined to defraud me of her, and I care for neither and defy them all. Kiku, Kiku, come to me!'

The pilgrim, thinking his cramped position would be dangerous if the maniac came near him, availed himself of an opportunity, when the latter was in a far-off part of the temple, to get out into the grounds and hide himself again. It would be easier to see what went on, thought he, and to run if necessary.

He hid himself first in one part of the grounds and then in another. Meanwhile, the mad priest paid several rushing visits to the outsides of the temple, keeping up all the time his awful cries for O-Kiku. Towards morning he retired once more to the part of the temple in which he lived, and no more noise was made. Our pilgrim then went forth from his hiding place, and seated himself on the rock which he had occupied the evening before, determined to see if he could not force a conversation with the demented man and read him a lesson from the sacred teachings of Buddha. He sat patiently on until the sun was high, but all remained silent. There was no sign of the mad priest.

Towards midday the pilgrim heard sounds in the temple; and, by and by, the madman came out, looking as if he had just recovered from a drunken orgy. He appeared dazed and was quiet, and started as he saw the old priest seated on the rock as he had been the night before. The old man rose and, approaching him, said:

'My friend, my name is Ungai. I am a brother priest – from the Temple of Daigoji in Wakasa Province. I came hither to see you, hearing of your great wisdom; but last night I heard in the village that you had broken your vows as a priest and lost your heart to a maiden, and that from love of her you have turned into a dangerous demon. I have in consequence considered it my duty to come and read you a lecture, as it is impossible to pass your conduct unnoticed. Pray, listen to the lecture and tell me if I can help you.'

The mad priest answered quite meekly:

'You are indeed a Buddha. Please tell me what I can do to forget the past, and to become a holy and virtuous priest once more.'

Ungai answered:

'Come out here into the grounds and seat yourself on this rock.' Then he read a lecture out of the Buddhist Bible, and finished by saying, 'And now, if you wish to redeem your soul, you must sit on this rock until you are able to explain the following lines, which are written in this sacred book: "*The moon on the lake shines on the winds between the pine trees, and a long night grows quiet at midnight!*"' Having said this, Ungai bowed low and left the mad priest, Joan, seated on the rock, reflecting.

For a month Ungai wandered from temple to temple, lecturing. At the end of that time he came back by way of Fumonji Temple, and thought he would go up to it and see what had happened to mad Joan. At the teahouse at which he had first put up, he asked the old landlady if she had seen or heard any more of the crazy priest.

'No,' she said, 'we have neither seen nor heard of him. Some people say he has left; but no one knows, for none dare go up to the temple to see.'

'Well,' said Ungai, 'I will go up tomorrow morning and find out.'

Next morning, Ungai went to the temple and found Joan still seated exactly as he had left him on the rock, muttering the words: '*The moon on the lake shines on the winds between the pine trees, and a long night grows quiet at midnight!*' Joan's hair and beard had become long and grey in the time, and he appeared to be miserably thin and almost transparent. Ungai was struck with pity at Joan's righteous determination and patience, and tears came to his eyes.

'Get up, get up,' said he, 'for indeed you are a holy and determined man.'

But Joan did not move. Ungai poked him with his staff, to awaken him, as he thought, but to his horror, Joan fell to pieces and disappeared like a flake of melting snow.

Ungai stayed in the temple for three days, praying for the soul of Joan. The villagers, hearing of this generous action, rebuilt the temple and made him their priest. Their temple had formerly belonged to the Mitsu sect, but now it was transferred to Ungai's 'Jo do' sect, and the title or name of 'Fumonji' was changed to 'Hakkotsuzan' (White Bone Mountain). The temple is said to have prospered for hundreds of years after.

R. G. S.
1908

Mujina

On the Akasaka Road in Tokyo there is a slope called Kii-no-kuni-zaka, which means the Slope of the Province of Kii. I do not know why it is called the Slope of the Province of Kii. On one side of this slope you see an ancient moat, deep and very wide, with high green banks rising up to some place of gardens – and on the other side of the road extend the long and lofty walls of an imperial palace. Before the era of street lamps and *jinriki-shas*, this neighbourhood was very lonesome after dark, and belated pedestrians would go miles out of their way rather than mount the Kii-no-kuni-zaka alone after sunset.

All because of a *Mujina* that used to walk there.

The last man who saw the *Mujina* was an old merchant of the Kyōbashi quarter, who died about thirty years ago. This is the story, as he told it: –

One night, at a late hour, he was hurrying up the Kii-no-kuni-zaka when he perceived a woman crouching by the moat, all alone and weeping bitterly. Fearing that she intended to drown herself, he stopped to offer her any assistance or consolation in his power. She appeared to be a slight and graceful person, handsomely dressed, and her hair was arranged like that of a young girl of good family.

'*O-jochū!*'* he exclaimed, approaching her. '*O-jochū*, do not cry like that! . . . Tell me what the trouble is and if there be any way to help you, I shall be glad to help you.' (He really meant what he said, for he was a very kind man.) But she continued to weep – hiding her face from him with one of her long sleeves.

'*O-jochū*,' he said again, as gently as he could, 'please, please listen to me! . . . This is no place for a young lady at night! Do not cry, I implore you! – only tell me how I may be of some help to you!'

Slowly she rose up, but turned her back to him, and continued to moan and sob behind her sleeve.

He laid his hand lightly upon her shoulder, and pleaded: '*O-jochū! – O-jochū! – O-jochū!* . . . Listen to me, just for one little moment! . . . *O-jochū! – O-jochū!*'

Then that *O-jochū* turned around and dropped her sleeve, and stroked her face with her hand – and the man saw that she had no eyes or nose or mouth – and he screamed and ran away.

Up Kii-no-kuni-zaka he ran and ran; and all was black and empty before him. On and on he ran, never daring to look back; and at last he saw a lantern, so far away that it looked like the gleam of a firefly; and he made for it. It proved to be only the lantern of an itinerant *soba*-seller, who had set down his stand by the roadside; but any light and any human companionship was good after that experience, and he flung himself down at the feet of the *soba*-seller, crying out, 'Ah! – aa!! – *aa!!!*' . . .

'*Koré! koré!*' roughly exclaimed the *soba*-man. 'Here! What is the matter with you? Anybody hurt you?'

'No – nobody hurt me,' panted the other – 'only . . . *Ah! – aa!*'

'Only scared you?' queried the peddler, unsympathetically. 'Robbers?'

---

* 'Honourable damsel!'

'Not robbers – not robbers,' gasped the terrified man. 'I saw . . . I saw a woman – by the moat – and she showed me . . . *Ah!* I cannot tell you what she showed me!'

'*Hé!* Was it anything like *this* that she showed you?' cried the *soba*-man, stroking his own face, which therewith became like unto an egg . . . And, simultaneously, the light went out.

L. H.
1904

A Passional Karma

One of the never-failing attractions of the Tokyo stage is the performance, by the famous Kikugorō and his company, of the *Botan-Dōrō* or *Peony-Lantern*. This weird play, of which the scenes are laid in the middle of the last century, is the dramatisation of a romance by the novelist Enchō, written in colloquial Japanese, and purely Japanese in local colour, though inspired by a Chinese tale. I went to see the play; and Kikugorō made me familiar with a new variety of the pleasure of fear.

'Why not give English readers the ghostly part of the story?' asked a friend who guides me betimes through the mazes of Eastern philosophy. 'It would serve to explain some popular ideas of the supernatural which Western people know very little about. And I could help you with the translation.'

I gladly accepted the suggestion; and we composed the following summary of the more extraordinary portion of Enchō's romance. Here and there, we found it necessary to condense the original narrative; and we tried to keep close to the text only in the conversational passages – some of which happen to possess a particular quality of psychological interest.

I

There once lived in the district of Ushigome in Tokyo, a *hatamoto*★ called Iijima Heizayémon, whose only daughter Tsuyu was beautiful as her name, which signifies 'Morning Dew'. Iijima took a second wife when his daughter was about sixteen; and, finding that O-Tsuyu could not be happy with her mother-in-law, he had a pretty villa built for the girl at Yanagijima, as a separate residence, and gave her an excellent maidservant called O-Yoné to wait upon her.

O-Tsuyu lived happily enough in her new home until one day when the family physician Yamamoto Shijō paid her a visit in company with a young samurai named Hagiwara Shinzaburō, who resided in the Nedzu quarter. Shinzaburō was an unusually handsome lad and very gentle; and the two young people fell in love with each other at sight. Even before the brief visit was over, they contrived – unheard by the old doctor – to pledge themselves to each other for life. And, at parting, O-Tsuyu whispered to the youth, 'Remember! If you do not come to see me again, I shall certainly die!'

Shinzaburō never forgot those words, and he was only too eager to see more of O-Tsuyu. But etiquette forbade him to make the visit alone: he was obliged to wait for some other chance to accompany the doctor, who had promised to take him to the villa a second time. Unfortunately, the old man did not keep this promise. He had perceived the sudden affection of O-Tsuyu and he feared that her father would hold him responsible for any serious results. Iijima Heizayémon had a reputation for cutting off heads. And the more Shijō thought about the possible consequences of his introduction of Shinzaburō at the

★ The *hatamoto* were samurai forming the special military force of the Shogun.

Iijima villa, the more he became afraid. Therefore, he purposely abstained from calling upon his young friend.

Months passed and O-Tsuyu, little imagining the true cause of Shinzaburō's neglect, believed that her love had been scorned. Then she pined away and died. Soon afterwards, the faithful servant O-Yoné also died through grief at the loss of her mistress; and the two were buried side by side in the cemetery of Shin-Banzui-In, a temple which still stands in the neighbourhood of Dango-Zaka, where the famous chrysanthemum shows are yearly held.

II

Shinzaburō knew nothing of what had happened, but his disappointment and his anxiety had resulted in a prolonged illness. He was slowly recovering, but still very weak, when he unexpectedly received another visit from Yamamoto Shijō. The old man made a number of plausible excuses for his apparent neglect. Shinzaburō said to him: 'I have been sick ever since the beginning of spring – even now I cannot eat anything . . . Was it not rather unkind of you never to call? I thought that we were to make another visit together to the house of the Lady Iijima, and I wanted to take to her some little present as a return for our kind reception. Of course I could not go by myself.'

Shijō gravely responded, 'I am very sorry to tell you that the young lady is dead!'

'Dead!' repeated Shinzaburō, turning white. 'Did you say that she is dead?'

The doctor remained silent for a moment, as if collecting himself: then he resumed, in the quick light tone of a man resolved not to take trouble seriously:

'My great mistake was in having introduced you to her, for it seems that she fell in love with you at once. I am afraid that you must have said something to encourage this affection – when you were in that little room together. At all events, I saw how she felt towards you, and then I became uneasy – fearing that her father might come to hear of the matter and lay the whole blame upon me. So – to be quite frank with you – I decided that it would be better not to call upon you, and I purposely stayed away for a long time. But only a few days ago, happening to visit Iijima's house, I heard, to my great surprise, that his daughter had died, and that her servant O-Yoné had also died. Then, remembering all that had taken place, I knew that the young lady must have died of love for you . . . (*Laughing*) Ah, you are really a sinful fellow! Yes, you are! (*Laughing*) Isn't it a sin to have been born so handsome that the girls die for love of you? (*Seriously*) Well, we must leave the dead to the dead. It is no use to talk further about the matter – all that you now can do for her is to repeat the *Nembutsu*★ . . . Goodbye.'

And the old man retired hastily – anxious to avoid further converse about the painful event for which he felt himself to have been unwittingly responsible.

III

Shinzaburō long remained stupefied with grief by the news of O-Tsuyu's death. But as soon as he found himself again able to think clearly, he inscribed the dead girl's name upon a mortuary tablet and placed the tablet in the Buddhist shrine of his

★ The invocation '*Namu Amida Butsu!*' ('Hail to the Buddha Amitâbha!') – repeated, as a prayer, for the sake of the dead.

house, and set offerings before it and recited prayers. Every day thereafter he presented offerings and repeated the *Nembutsu*; and the memory of O-Tsuyu was never absent from his thought.

Nothing occurred to change the monotony of his solitude before the time of the Bon – the great Festival of the Dead – which begins upon the thirteenth day of the seventh month. Then he decorated his house and prepared everything for the festival – hanging out the lanterns that guide the returning spirits, and setting the food of ghosts on the *shōryōdana* or Shelf of Souls. And on the first evening of the Bon, after sundown, he kindled a small lamp before the tablet of O-Tsuyu and lighted the lanterns.

The night was clear, with a great moon – and windless and very warm. Shinzaburō sought the coolness of his veranda. Clad only in a light summer robe, he sat there, thinking, dreaming, sorrowing – sometimes fanning himself, sometimes making a little smoke to drive the mosquitoes away. Everything was quiet. It was a lonesome neighbourhood and there were few passers-by. He could hear only the soft rushing of a neighbouring stream and the shrilling of night insects.

But all at once this stillness was broken by a sound of women's *geta* (clogs) approaching – *kara-kon, kara-kon* – and the sound drew nearer and nearer, quickly, till it reached the live hedge surrounding the garden. Then Shinzaburō, feeling curious, stood on tiptoe, so as to look over the hedge; and he saw two women passing. One, who was carrying a beautiful lantern decorated with peony flowers, appeared to be a servant – the other was a slender girl of about seventeen, wearing a long-sleeved robe embroidered with designs of autumn blossoms. Almost at the same instant both women turned their faces towards Shinzaburō – and to his utter astonishment he recognised O-Tsuyu and her servant O-Yoné.

They stopped immediately and the girl cried out, 'Oh, how strange! . . . Hagiwara Sama!'

Shinzaburō simultaneously called to the maid: 'O-Yoné! Ah, you are O-Yoné! – I remember you very well.'

'Hagiwara Sama!' exclaimed O-Yoné in a tone of supreme amazement. 'Never could I have believed it possible! . . . Sir, we were told that you had died.'

'How extraordinary!' cried Shinzaburō. 'Why, I was told that both of you were dead!'

'Ah, what a hateful story!' returned O-Yoné. 'Why repeat such unlucky words? . . . Who told you?'

'Please do come in,' said Shinzaburō. 'Here we can talk better. The garden gate is open.'

So they entered and exchanged greeting; and when Shinzaburō had made them comfortable, he said:

'I trust that you will pardon my discourtesy in not having called upon you for so long a time. But Shijō, the doctor, about a month ago, told me that you had both died.'

'So it was he who told you?' exclaimed O-Yoné. 'It was very wicked of him to say such a thing. Well, it was also Shijō who told us that *you* were dead. I think that he wanted to deceive you – which was not a difficult thing to do, because you are so confiding and trustful. Possibly my mistress betrayed her liking for you in some words which found their way to her father's ears; and, in that case, O-Kuni – the new wife – might have planned to make the doctor tell you that we were dead, so as to bring about a separation. Anyhow, when my mistress heard that you had died she wanted to cut off her hair immediately and to become a nun. But I was able to prevent her from cutting off her hair and I persuaded her at last to become a nun only in her heart. Afterwards, her father wished her to marry a certain young man and she refused. Then there was a great deal of trouble – chiefly caused by O-Kuni – and we went away from

the villa and found a very small house in Yanaka-no-Sasaki.
There we are now just barely able to live, by doing a little private work . . . My mistress has been constantly repeating the
Nembutsu for your sake. Today, being the first day of the Bon,
we went to visit the temples; and we were on our way home –
thus late – when this strange meeting happened.'

'Oh, how extraordinary!' cried Shinzaburō. 'Can it be true?
Or is it only a dream? Here I, too, have been constantly reciting
the *Nembutsu* before a tablet with her name upon it! Look!' And
he showed them O-Tsuyu's tablet in its place upon the Shelf of
Souls.

'We are more than grateful for your kind remembrance,'
returned O-Yoné, smiling. 'Now as for my mistress,' she
continued – turning towards O-Tsuyu, who had all the while
remained demure and silent, half-hiding her face with her
sleeve – 'as for my mistress, she actually says that she would not
mind being disowned by her father for the time of seven existences, or even being killed by him, for your sake! Come! Will
you not allow her to stay here tonight?'

Shinzaburō turned pale for joy. He answered in a voice trembling with emotion:

'Please remain, but do not speak loud – because there is a
troublesome fellow living close by – a *ninsomi* (fortune teller)
called Hakuōdō Yusai, who tells people's fortunes by looking at
their faces. He is inclined to be curious, and it is better that he
should not know.'

The two women remained that night in the house of the
young samurai, and returned to their own home a little before
daybreak. And after that night they came every night for seven
nights, – whether the weather were foul or fair – always at the
same hour. And Shinzaburō became more and more attached to
the girl; and the twain were fettered, each to each, by that bond
of illusion which is stronger than bands of iron.

IV

Now there was a man called Tomozō, who lived in a small cottage adjoining Shinzaburō's residence. Tomozō and his wife O-Miné were both employed by Shinzaburō as servants. Both seemed to be devoted to their young master; and by his help they were able to live in comparative comfort.

One night, at a very late hour, Tomozō heard the voice of a woman in his master's apartment; and this made him uneasy. He feared that Shinzaburō, being very gentle and affectionate, might be made the dupe of some cunning wanton – in which event the domestics would be the first to suffer. He therefore resolved to watch; and on the following night he stole on tiptoe to Shinzaburō's dwelling and looked through a chink in one of the sliding shutters. By the glow of a night lantern within the sleeping-room, he was able to perceive that his master and a strange woman were talking together under the mosquito net. At first he could not see the woman distinctly. Her back was turned to him – he only observed that she was very slim and that she appeared to be very young – judging from the fashion of her dress and hair. Putting his ear to the chink, he could hear the conversation plainly. The woman said:

'And if I should be disowned by my father, would you then let me come and live with you?'

Shinzaburō answered:

'Most assuredly I would – nay, I should be glad of the chance. But there is no reason to fear that you will ever be disowned by your father; for you are his only daughter and he loves you very much. What I do fear is that some day we shall be cruelly separated.'

She responded softly:

'Never, never could I even think of accepting any other man

for my husband. Even if our secret were to become known, and my father were to kill me for what I have done, still – after death itself – I could never cease to think of you. And I am now quite sure that you yourself would not be able to live very long without me.' . . . Then, clinging closely to him, with her lips at his neck, she caressed him, and he returned her caresses.

Tomozō wondered as he listened – because the language of the woman was not the language of a common woman, but the language of a lady of rank. Then he determined at all hazards to get one glimpse of her face; and he crept around the house, backwards and forwards, peering through every crack and chink. And at last he was able to see – but therewith an icy trembling seized him and the hair of his head stood up.

For the face was the face of a woman long dead – and the fingers caressing were fingers of naked bone – and of the body below the waist there was not anything: it melted off into thinnest trailing shadow. Where the eyes of the deluded lover saw youth and grace and beauty, there appeared to the eyes of the watcher horror only, and the emptiness of death. Simultaneously, another woman's figure, and a weirder, rose up from within the chamber and swiftly made towards the watcher, as if discerning his presence. Then, in uttermost terror, he fled to the dwelling of Hakuōdō Yusai, and, knocking frantically at the doors, succeeded in arousing him.

V

Hakuōdō Yusai, the *ninsomi*, was a very old man; but in his time he had travelled much, and he had heard and seen so many things that he could not be easily surprised. Yet the story of the terrified Tomozō both alarmed and amazed him. He had read in ancient Chinese books of love between the living and the dead, but he had never believed it possible. Now, however, he felt convinced that the statement of Tomozō was not a falsehood, and that something very strange was really going on in the house of Hagiwara. Should the truth prove to be what Tomozō imagined, then the young samurai was a doomed man.

'If the woman be a ghost,' said Yusai to the frightened servant, 'if the woman be a ghost, your master must die very soon – unless something extraordinary can be done to save him. And if the woman be a ghost, the signs of death will appear upon his face. For the spirit of the living is *yōki* and pure – the spirit of the dead is *inki* and unclean: the one is positive, the other negative. He whose bride is a ghost cannot live. Even though in his blood there existed the force of a life of one hundred years, that force must quickly perish . . . Still, I shall do all that I can to save Hagiwara Sama. And in the meantime, Tomozō, say nothing to any other person – not even to your wife – about this matter. At sunrise I shall call upon your master.'

VI

When questioned next morning by Yusai, Shinzaburō at first attempted to deny that any women had been visiting the house; but finding this artless policy of no avail, and perceiving that the old man's purpose was altogether unselfish, he was finally persuaded to acknowledge what had really occurred, and to give his reasons for wishing to keep the matter a secret. As for the lady Iijima, he intended, he said, to make her his wife as soon as possible.

'Oh, madness!' cried Yusai, losing all patience in the intensity of his alarm. 'Know, sir, that the people who have been coming here, night after night, are dead! Some frightful delusion is upon you! . . . Why, the simple fact that you long supposed O-Tsuyu to be dead, and repeated the *Nembutsu* for her, and made offerings before her tablet, is itself the proof! . . . The lips of the dead have touched you! The hands of the dead have caressed you! . . . Even at this moment I see in your face the signs of death – and you will not believe! . . . Listen to me now, sir – I beg of you – if you wish to save yourself: otherwise you have less than twenty days to live. They told you – those people – that they were residing in the district of Shitaya in Yanaka-no-Sasaki. Did you ever visit them at that place? No! – of course you did not! Then go today – as soon as you can – to Yanaka-no-Sasaki and try to find their home!'

And, having uttered this counsel with the most vehement earnestness, Hakuōdō Yusai abruptly took his departure.

Shinzaburō, startled though not convinced, resolved after a moment's reflection to follow the advice of the *ninsomi* and to go to Shitaya. It was yet early in the morning when he reached the quarter of Yanaka-no-Sasaki and began his search for the dwelling of O-Tsuyu. He went through every street and side street, read all the names inscribed at the various entrances, and made inquiries whenever an opportunity presented itself. But he could not find anything resembling the little house mentioned by O-Yoné; and none of the people whom he questioned knew of any house in the quarter inhabited by two single women. Feeling at last certain that further research would be useless, he turned homeward by the shortest way, which happened to lead through the grounds of the temple Shin-Banzui-In.

Suddenly his attention was attracted by two new tombs, placed side by side, at the rear of the temple. One was a common tomb, such as might have been erected for a person of humble rank: the other was a large and handsome monument; and hanging before it was a beautiful peony-lantern, which had probably been left there at the time of the Festival of the Dead. Shinzaburō remembered that the peony-lantern carried by O-Yoné was exactly similar, and the coincidence impressed him as strange.

He looked again at the tombs, but the tombs explained nothing. Neither bore any personal name – only the Buddhist *kaimyō* or posthumous appellation. Then he determined to seek information at the temple. An acolyte stated, in reply to his questions, that the large tomb had been recently erected for the daughter of Iijima Heizayémon, the *hatamoto* of Ushigome; and that the small tomb next to it was that of her servant O-Yoné, who had died of grief soon after the young lady's funeral.

Immediately to Shinzaburō's memory there recurred, with another and sinister meaning, the words of O-Yoné: '*We went away, and found a very small house in Yanaka-no-Sasaki. There we are now just barely able to live – by doing a little private work . . .*' Here was indeed the very small house – and in Yanaka-no-Sasaki. But the little *private work . . .* ?

Terror-stricken, the samurai hastened with all speed to the house of Yusai, and begged for his counsel and assistance. But Yusai declared himself unable to be of any aid in such a case. All that he could do was to send Shinzaburō to the high priest Ryōseki of Shin-Banzui-In, with a letter praying for immediate religious help.

VII

The high priest Ryōseki was a learned and a holy man. By spiritual vision he was able to know the secret of any sorrow, and the nature of the karma that had caused it. He heard, unmoved, the story of Shinzaburō, and said to him:

'A very great danger now threatens you, because of an error committed in one of your former states of existence. The karma that binds you to the dead is very strong; but if I tried to explain its character, you would not be able to understand. I shall therefore tell you only this – that the dead person has no desire to injure you out of hate, feels no enmity towards you: she is influenced, on the contrary, by the most passionate affection for you. Probably the girl has been in love with you from a time long preceding your present life – from a time of not less than three or four past existences; and it would seem that, although necessarily changing her form and condition at each succeeding birth, she has not been able to cease from following after you. Therefore, it will not be an easy thing to escape from her influence . . . But now I am going to lend you this powerful *mamori*. It is a pure gold image of the Buddha called the Sea-Sounding Tathâgata – *Kai-On-Nyōrai* – because his preaching of the Law sounds through the world like the sound of the sea. And this little image is especially a *shiryō-yoké*, which protects the living from the dead. This you must wear, in its covering, next to your body, under the girdle . . . Besides, I shall presently perform in the temple a *Ségaki*-service* for the repose of the troubled spirit . . . And here is a holy sutra called *Ubō-Darani-Kyō* or 'Treasure-raining Sutra'. You must be careful to recite it every night in your house – without fail . . . Furthermore, I shall give you this package of *o-fuda* (paper talismans) – you must paste one of them over every opening of your house – no matter how small. If you do this, the power of the holy texts will prevent the dead from entering. But – whatever may happen – do not fail to recite the sutra.'

Shinzaburō humbly thanked the high priest; and then, taking with him the image, the sutra and the bundle of sacred texts, he made all haste to reach his home before the hour of sunset.

---

* A special Buddhist service to those dead having no living relatives or friends to care for them.

VIII

With Yusai's advice and help, Shinzaburō was able before dark to fix the holy texts over all the apertures of his dwelling. Then the *ninsomi* returned to his own house, leaving the youth alone.

Night came, warm and clear. Shinzaburō made fast the doors, bound the precious amulet about his waist, entered his mosquito net, and by the glow of a night lantern began to recite the *Ubō-Darani-Kyō*. For a long time he chanted the words, comprehending little of their meaning; then he tried to obtain some rest. But his mind was still too much disturbed by the strange events of the day. Midnight passed and no sleep came to him. At last he heard the boom of the great temple bell of Dentsu-In announcing the eighth hour.*

It ceased and Shinzaburō suddenly heard the sound of *geta* approaching from the old direction – but this time more slowly: *karan-koron, karan-koron!* At once a cold sweat broke over his forehead. Opening the sutra hastily, with trembling hand, he began again to recite it aloud. The steps came nearer and nearer – reached the live hedge – stopped! Then, strange to say, Shinzaburō felt unable to remain under his mosquito net: something stronger even than his fear impelled him to look; and, instead of continuing to recite the *Ubō-Darani-Kyō*, he foolishly approached the shutters and through a chink peered out into the night. Before the house he saw O-Tsuyu standing, and O-Yoné with the peony-lantern; and both of them were gazing at the Buddhist texts pasted above the entrance. Never before – not

---

* According to the old Japanese way of counting time, this *yatsudoki* or eighth hour was the same as our two o'clock in the morning. Each Japanese hour was equal to two European hours, so that there were only six hours instead of our twelve; and these six hours were counted backwards in the order 9, 8, 7, 6, 5, 4. Two o'clock in the morning, also called 'The Hour of the Ox', was the Japanese hour of ghosts and goblins.

even in what little time she lived – had O-Tsuyu appeared so beautiful; and Shinzaburō felt his heart drawn towards her with a power almost resistless. But the terror of death and the terror of the unknown restrained him; and there went on within him such a struggle between his love and his fear that he became as one suffering in the body the pains of the Shō-netsu hell.★

Presently, he heard the voice of the maidservant, saying:

'My dear mistress, there is no way to enter. The heart of Hagiwara Sama must have changed. For the promise that he made last night has been broken; and the doors have been made fast to keep us out . . . We cannot go in tonight . . . It will be wiser for you to make up your mind not to think any more about him, because his feeling towards you has certainly changed. It is evident that he does not want to see you. So it will be better not to give yourself any more trouble for the sake of a man whose heart is so unkind.'

But the girl answered, weeping:

'Oh, to think that this could happen after the pledges which we made to each other! . . . Often I was told that the heart of a man changes as quickly as the sky of autumn – yet surely the heart of Hagiwara Sama cannot be so cruel that he should really intend to exclude me in this way! . . . Dear Yoné, please find some means of taking me to him . . . Unless you do, I will never, never go home again.'

Thus she continued to plead, veiling her face with her long sleeves – and very beautiful she looked, and very touching; but the fear of death was strong upon her lover.

O-Yoné at last made answer, 'My dear young lady, why will you trouble your mind about a man who seems to be so cruel? . . .

★ The sixth of the Eight Hot Hells of Japanese Buddhism. One day of life in this hell is equal in duration to thousands (some say millions) of human years.

Well, let us see if there be no way to enter at the back of the house: come with me!'

And taking O-Tsuyu by the hand, she led her away towards the rear of the dwelling; and there the two disappeared as suddenly as the light disappears when the flame of a lamp is blown out.

IX

Night after night the shadows came at the Hour of the Ox; and, nightly, Shinzaburō heard the weeping of O-Tsuyu. Yet he believed himself saved, little imagining that his doom had already been decided by the character of his dependants.

Tomozō had promised Yusai never to speak to any other person — not even to O-Miné — of the strange events that were taking place. But Tomozō was not long suffered by the haunters to rest in peace. Night after night, O-Yoné entered into his dwelling and roused him from his sleep, and asked him to remove the *o-fuda* placed over one very small window at the back of his master's house. And Tomozō, out of fear, as often promised her to take away the *o-fuda* before the next sundown; but never by day could he make up his mind to remove it, believing that evil was intended to Shinzaburō. At last, in a night of storm, O-Yoné startled him from slumber with a cry of reproach, and stooped above his pillow and said to him: 'Have a care how you trifle with us! If by tomorrow night you do not take away that text, you shall learn how I can hate!' And she made her face so frightful as she spoke that Tomozō nearly died of terror.

O-Miné, the wife of Tomozō, had never till then known of these visits: even to her husband they had seemed like bad dreams. But on this particular night it chanced that, waking suddenly, she heard the voice of a woman talking to Tomozō.

Almost in the same moment the talking ceased; and when O-Miné looked about her, she saw, by the light of the night lamp, only her husband, shuddering and white with fear. The stranger was gone; the doors were fast: it seemed impossible that anybody could have entered. Nevertheless, the jealousy of the wife had been aroused; and she began to chide and to question Tomozō in such a manner that he thought himself obliged to betray the secret, and to explain the terrible dilemma in which he had been placed.

Then the passion of O-Miné yielded to wonder and alarm; but she was a subtle woman and she devised immediately a plan to save her husband by the sacrifice of her master. And she gave Tomozō a cunning counsel, telling him to make conditions with the dead.

They came again on the following night at the Hour of the Ox; and O-Miné hid herself on hearing the sound of their coming, *karan-koron, karan-koron!* But Tomozō went out to meet them in the dark, and even found courage to say to them what his wife had told him to say:

'It is true that I deserve your blame, but I had no wish to cause you anger. The reason that the *o-fuda* has not been taken away is that my wife and I are able to live only by the help of Hagiwara Sama, and that we cannot expose him to any danger without bringing misfortune upon ourselves. But if we could obtain the sum of 100 *ryō* in gold, we should be able to please you, because we should then need no help from anybody. Therefore, if you will give us 100 *ryō*, I can take the *o-fuda* away without being afraid of losing our only means of support.'

When he had uttered these words, O-Yoné and O-Tsuyu looked at each other in silence for a moment. Then O-Yoné said:

'Mistress, I told you that it was not right to trouble this man, as we have no just cause of ill will against him. But it is certainly useless to fret yourself about Hagiwara Sama, because his heart has changed towards you. Now once again, my dear young lady, let me beg you not to think any more about him!'

But O-Tsuyu, weeping, made answer:

'Dear Yoné, whatever may happen, I cannot possibly keep myself from thinking about him! You know that you can get 100 *ryō* to have the *o-fuda* taken off . . . Only once more, I pray, dear Yoné! Only once more bring me face to face with Hagiwara Sama – I beseech you!' And, hiding her face with her sleeve, she thus continued to plead.

'Oh! why will you ask me to do these things?' responded O-Yoné. 'You know very well that I have no money. But since you will persist in this whim of yours, in spite of all that I can say, I suppose that I must try to find the money somehow, and to bring it here tomorrow night.' Then, turning to the faithless Tomozō, she said: 'Tomozō, I must tell you that Hagiwara Sama now wears upon his body a *mamori* called by the name of *Kai-On-Nyōrai*, and that so long as he wears it we cannot approach him. So you will have to get that *mamori* away from him, by some means or other, as well as to remove the *o-fuda*.'

Tomozō feebly made answer:

'That also I can do, if you will promise to bring me the 100 *ryō*.'

'Well, mistress,' said O-Yoné, 'you will wait, will you not, until tomorrow night?'

'Oh, dear Yoné!' sobbed the other. 'Have we to go back tonight again without seeing Hagiwara Sama? Ah! it is cruel!'

And the shadow of the mistress, weeping, was led away by the shadow of the maid.

X

Another day went and another night came, and the dead came with it. But this time no lamentation was heard without the house of Hagiwara; for the faithless servant found his reward at the Hour of the Ox and removed the *o-fuda*. Moreover, he had been able, while his master was at the bath, to steal from its case the golden *mamori* and to substitute for it an image of copper; and he had buried the *Kai-On-Nyōrai* in a desolate field. So the visitants found nothing to oppose their entering. Veiling their faces with their sleeves, they rose and passed like a streaming of vapour into the little window from over which the holy text had been torn away. But what happened thereafter within the house Tomozō never knew.

The sun was high before he ventured again to approach his master's dwelling and to knock upon the sliding doors. For the first time in years he obtained no response; and the silence made him afraid. Repeatedly, he called and received no answer. Then, aided by O-Miné, he succeeded in effecting an entrance and making his way alone to the sleeping-room, where he called again in vain. He rolled back the rumbling shutters to admit the light, but still within the house there was no stir. At last he dared to lift a corner of the mosquito net. But no sooner had he looked beneath than he fled from the house with a cry of horror.

Shinzaburō was dead – hideously dead – and his face was the face of a man who had died in the uttermost agony of fear – and lying beside him in the bed were the bones of a woman! And the bones of the arms, and the bones of the hands, clung fast about his neck.

XI

Hakuōdō Yusai, the fortune teller, went to view the corpse at the prayer of the faithless Tomozō. The old man was terrified and astonished at the spectacle, but looked about him with a keen eye. He soon perceived that the *o-fuda* had been taken from the little window at the back of the house; and, on searching the body of Shinzaburō, he discovered that the golden *mamori* had been taken from its wrapping and a copper image of Fudō put in place of it. He suspected Tomozō of the theft, but the whole occurrence was so very extraordinary that he thought it prudent to consult with the priest Ryōseki before taking further action. Therefore, after having made a careful examination of the premises, he betook himself to the temple Shin-Banzui-In as quickly as his aged limbs could bear him.

Ryōseki, without waiting to hear the purpose of the old man's visit, at once invited him into a private apartment.

'You know that you are always welcome here,' said Ryōseki. 'Please seat yourself at ease . . . Well, I am sorry to tell you that Hagiwara Sama is dead.'

Yusai wonderingly exclaimed: 'Yes, he is dead – but how did you learn of it?'

The priest responded:

'Hagiwara Sama was suffering from the results of an evil karma; and his attendant was a bad man. What happened to Hagiwara Sama was unavoidable – his destiny had been determined from a time long before his last birth. It will be better for you not to let your mind be troubled by this event.'

Yusai said:

'I have heard that a priest of pure life may gain power to see into the future for a hundred years, but truly this is the first time in my existence that I have had proof of such power . . . Still, there is another matter about which I am very anxious.'

'You mean,' interrupted Ryōseki, 'the stealing of the holy *mamori*, the *Kai-On-Nyōrai*. But you must not give yourself any concern about that. The image has been buried in a field, and it will be found there and returned to me during the eighth month of the coming year. So please do not be anxious about it.'

More and more amazed, the old *ninsomi* ventured to observe:

'I have studied the *In-Yō*★ and the science of divination, and I make my living by telling people's fortunes – but I cannot possibly understand how you know these things.'

Ryōseki answered gravely:

'Never mind how I happen to know them . . . I now want to speak to you about Hagiwara's funeral. The House of Hagiwara has its own family cemetery, of course, but to bury him there would not be proper. He must be buried beside O-Tsuyu, the Lady Iijima, for his karma-relation to her was a very deep one. And it is but right that you should erect a tomb for him at your own cost, because you have been indebted to him for many favours.'

Thus it came to pass that Shinzaburō was buried beside O-Tsuyu in the cemetery of Shin-Banzui-In, in Yanaka-no-Sasaki.

Here ends the story of the ghosts in the romance of the Peony-Lantern.

★

My friend asked me whether the story had interested me, and I answered by telling him that I wanted to go to the cemetery of Shin-Banzui-In, so as to realise more definitely the local colour of the author's studies.

'I shall go with you at once,' he said. 'But what did you think of the personages?'

'To Western thinking,' I made answer, 'Shinzaburō is a despicable creature. I have been mentally comparing him with the true lovers of our old ballad literature. They were only too glad to follow a dead sweetheart into the grave; and, nevertheless, being Christians, they believed that they had only one human life to enjoy in this world. But Shinzaburō was a

★ The Male and Female principles of the universe, the Active and Passive forces of Nature.

Buddhist with a million lives behind him and a million lives before him; and he was too selfish to give up even one miserable existence for the sake of the girl that came back to him from the dead. Then he was even more cowardly than selfish. Although a samurai by birth and training, he had to beg a priest to save him from ghosts. In every way he proved himself contemptible, and O-Tsuyu did quite right in choking him to death.'

'From the Japanese point of view, likewise,' my friend responded, 'Shinzaburō is rather contemptible. But the use of this weak character helped the author to develop incidents that could not otherwise, perhaps, have been so effectively managed. To my thinking, the only attractive character in the story is that of O-Yoné: a type of the old-time loyal and loving servant – intelligent, shrewd, full of resource – faithful not only unto death, but beyond death . . . Well, let us go to Shin-Banzui-In.'

We found the temple uninteresting, and the cemetery an abomination of desolation. Spaces once occupied by graves had been turned into potato patches. Between were tombs leaning at all angles out of the perpendicular, tablets made illegible by scurf, empty pedestals, shattered water tanks, and statues of Buddhas without heads or hands. Recent rains had soaked the black soil, leaving here and there small pools of slime about which swarms of tiny frogs were hopping. Everything – excepting the potato patches – seemed to have been neglected for years. In a shed just within the gate we observed a woman cooking; and my companion presumed to ask her if she knew anything about the tombs described in the romance of the *Peony-Lantern*.

'Ah! the tombs of O-Tsuyu and O-Yoné?' she responded, smiling. 'You will find them near the end of the first row at the back of the temple – next to the statue of Jizo.'

Surprises of this kind I had met with elsewhere in Japan.

We picked our way between the rain-pools and between the green ridges of young potatoes – whose roots were doubtless feeding on the substance of many another O-Tsuyu and O-Yoné – and we reached at last two lichen-eaten tombs of which the inscriptions seemed almost obliterated. Beside the larger tomb was a statue of Jizo with a broken nose.

'The characters are not easy to make out,' said my friend, 'but wait!' He drew from his sleeve a sheet of soft white paper, laid it over the inscription and began to rub the paper with a lump of clay. As he did so, the characters appeared in white on the blackened surface.

'*Eleventh day, third month – Rat, Elder Brother, Fire – Sixth year of Horéki* (1756 AD) . . . This would seem to be the grave of some innkeeper of Nedzu, named Kichibei. Let us see what is on the other monument.'

With a fresh sheet of paper he presently brought out the text of a *kaimyō*, and read:

'*En-myō-In, Hō-yō-I-tei-ken-shi, Hō-ni: – Nun-of-the-Law, Illustrious, Pure-of-heart-and-will, Famed-in-the-Law, inhabiting the Mansion-of-the-Preaching-of-Wonder* . . . The grave of some Buddhist nun.'

'What utter humbug!' I exclaimed. 'That woman was only making fun of us.'

'Now,' my friend protested, 'you are unjust to the woman! You came here because you wanted a sensation, and she tried her very best to please you. You did not suppose that ghost story was true, did you?'

L. H.
1899

Ghost Story of the Flute's Tomb

Long ago, at a small and out-of-the-way village called Kumeda-mura, about eight miles to the south-east of Sakai city in Idsumo Province, there was made a tomb, the *Fuezuka* or The Flute's Tomb, and to this day many people go thither to offer up prayer and to worship, bringing with them flowers and incense sticks, which are deposited as offerings to the spirit of the man who was buried there. All the year round people flock to it. There is no season at which they pray more particularly than at another.

The *Fuezuka* Tomb is situated on a large pond called Kumeda, some five miles in circumference, and all the places around this pond are known as of Kumeda Pond, from which the village of Kumeda took its name.

Whose tomb can it be that attracts such sympathy? The tomb itself is a simple stone pillar with nothing artistic to recommend it. Neither is the surrounding scenery interesting; it is flat and ugly until the mountains of Kiushu are reached. I must tell, as well as I can, the story of whose tomb it is.

Between seventy and eighty years ago there lived near the pond in the village of Kumedamura a blind *amma* (shampooer) called Yoichi. Yoichi was extremely popular in the neighbour-hood, being very honest and kind, besides being quite a professor in the art of massage — a treatment necessary to almost every

Japanese. It would be difficult indeed to find a village that had not its *amma*.

Yoichi was blind and, like all men of his calling, carried an iron wand or stick, also a flute or *fuezuka* – the stick to feel his way about with, and the flute to let people know he was ready for employment. So good an *amma* was Yoichi, he was nearly always employed, and, consequently, fairly well off, having a little house of his own and one servant, who cooked his food.

A little way from Yoichi's house was a small teahouse, placed upon the banks of the pond. One evening (the 5th of April, cherry-blossom season), just at dusk, Yoichi was on his way home, having been at work all day. His road led him by the pond. There he heard a girl crying piteously. He stopped and listened for a few moments, and gathered from what he heard that the girl was about to drown herself. Just as she entered the lake, Yoichi caught her by the dress and dragged her out.

'Who are you, and why in such trouble as to wish to die?' he asked.

'I am Asayo, the teahouse girl,' she answered. 'You know me quite well. You must know, also that it is not possible for me to support myself out of the small pittance which is paid by my master. I have eaten nothing for two days now, and am tired of my life.'

'Come, come!' said the blind man. 'Dry your tears. I will take you to my house and do what I can to help you. You are only twenty-five years of age, and I am told still a fair-looking girl. Perhaps you will marry! In any case, I will take care of you, and you must not think of killing yourself. Come with me now and I will see that you are well fed and that dry clothes are given you.'

So Yoichi led Asayo to his home.

A few months found them wedded to each other. Were they happy? Well, they should have been, for Yoichi treated his wife with the greatest kindness; but she was unlike her husband. She was selfish, bad-tempered and unfaithful. In the eyes of Japanese, infidelity is the worst of sins. How much more, then, is it against the country's spirit when advantage is taken of a husband who is blind?

Some three months after they had been married, and in the heat of August, there came to the village a company of actors. Among them was Sawamura Tamataro, of some repute in Asakusa.

Asayo, who was very fond of a play, spent much of her time and her husband's money in going to the theatre. In less than two days she had fallen violently in love with Tamataro. She sent him money, hard earned by her blind husband. She wrote to him love letters, begged him to allow her to come and visit him, and generally disgraced her sex.

Things went from bad to worse. The secret meetings of Asayo and the actor scandalised the neighbourhood. As in most such cases, the husband knew nothing about them. Frequently, when he went home, the actor was in his house, but kept quiet, and Asayo let him out secretly, even going with him sometimes.

Everyone felt sorry for Yoichi, but none liked to tell him of his wife's infidelity.

One day Yoichi went to shampoo a customer, who told him of Asayo's conduct. Yoichi was incredulous.

'But yes: it is true,' said the son of his customer. 'Even now the actor Tamataro is with your wife. So soon as you left your house he slipped in. This he does every day, and many of us see it. We all feel sorry for you in your blindness, and should be glad to help you to punish her.'

Yoichi was deeply grieved, for he knew that his friends were in earnest; but, though blind, he would accept no assistance to convict his wife. He trudged home as fast as his blindness would permit, making as little noise as possible with his staff.

On reaching home Yoichi found the front door fastened from

the inside. He went to the back and found the same thing there. There was no way of getting in without breaking a door and making a noise. Yoichi was much excited now, for he knew that his guilty wife and her lover were inside, and he would have liked to kill them both. Great strength came to him and he raised himself bit by bit until he reached the top of the roof. He intended to enter the house by letting himself down through the *tem-mado*.* Unfortunately, the straw rope he used in doing this was rotten and gave way, precipitating him below, where he fell on the *kinuta*†. He fractured his skull and died instantly.

Asayo and the actor, hearing the noise, went to see what had happened, and were rather pleased to find poor Yoichi dead. They did not report the death until next day, when they said that Yoichi had fallen downstairs and thus killed himself.

They buried him with indecent haste, and hardly with proper respect.

Yoichi having no children, his property, according to the Japanese law, went to his bad wife, and only a few months passed before Asayo and the actor were married. Apparently, they were happy, though none in the village of Kumeda had any sympathy for them, all being disgusted at their behaviour to the poor, blind shampooer Yoichi.

Months passed by without event of any interest in the village. No one bothered about Asayo and her husband; and they bothered about no one else, being sufficiently interested in themselves. The scandalmongers had become tired, and, like all nine-day wonders, the history of the blind *amma*, Asayo and Tamataro had passed into silence.

However, it does not do to be assured while the spirit of the injured dead goes unavenged.

---

* A hole in the roof of a Japanese house, in place of a chimney.
† A hard block of wood used in stretching cotton cloth.

Up in one of the western provinces, at a small village called Minato, lived one of Yoichi's friends, who was closely connected with him. This was Okuda Ichibei. He and Yoichi had been to school together. They had promised when Ichibei went up to the north-west always to remember each other, and to help each other in time of need, and when Yoichi had become blind, Ichibei came down to Kumeda and helped to start Yoichi in his business of *amma*, which he did by giving him a house to live in – a house which had been bequeathed to Ichibei. Again fate decreed that it should be in Ichibei's power to help his friend. At that time news travelled very slowly and Ichibei had not immediately heard of Yoichi's death or even of his marriage. Judge, then, of his surprise, one night on awaking, to find, standing near his pillow, the figure of a man whom by and by he recognised as Yoichi!

'Why, Yoichi! I am glad to see you,' he said, 'but how late at night you have arrived! Why did you not let me know you were coming? I should have been up to receive you and there would have been a hot meal ready. But never mind. I will call a servant and everything shall be ready as soon as possible. In the meantime, be seated and tell me about yourself and how you travelled so far. To have come through the mountains and other wild country from Kumeda is hard enough at best, but for one who is blind it is wonderful.'

'I am no longer a living man,' answered the ghost of Yoichi (for such it was). 'I am indeed your friend Yoichi's spirit, and I shall wander about until I can be avenged for a great ill which has been done me. I have come to beg of you to help me, that my spirit may go to rest. If you listen I will tell my story and you can then do as you think best.'

Ichibei was very much astonished (not to say a little nervous) to know that he was in the presence of a ghost; but he was a brave man and Yoichi had been his friend. He was deeply grieved to hear of Yoichi's death and realised that the restlessness of his spirit showed him to have been injured. Ichibei decided not only to listen to the story, but also to avenge Yoichi, and said so.

The ghost then told all that had happened since he had been set up in the house at Kumedamura. He told of his success as a masseur; of how he had saved the life of Asayo; how he had taken her to his house and subsequently married her; of the arrival of the accursed acting company which contained the man who had ruined his life; of his own death and hasty burial; and of the marriage of Asayo and the actor.

'I must be avenged. Will you help me to rest in peace?' he said in conclusion.

Ichibei promised. Then the spirit of Yoichi disappeared and Ichibei slept again.

Next morning Ichibei thought he must have been dreaming, but he remembered the vision and the narrative so clearly that he perceived them to have been actual. Suddenly turning with the intention to get up, he caught sight of the shine of a metal flute close to his pillow. It was the flute of a blind *amma*. It was marked with Yoichi's name.

Ichibei resolved to start for Kumedamura and ascertain locally all about Yoichi.

In those times, when there was no railway and a rickshaw only here and there, travel was slow. Ichibei took ten days to reach Kumedamura. He immediately went to the house of his friend Yoichi, and was there told the whole history again, but naturally in another way. Asayo said:

'Yes: he saved my life. We were married and I helped my blind husband in everything. One day, alas, he mistook the staircase for a door, falling down and killing himself. Now I am married to his great friend, an actor called Tamataro, whom you see here.'

Ichibei knew that the ghost of Yoichi was not likely to tell him lies and to ask for vengeance unjustly. Therefore, he continued talking to Asayo and her husband, listening to their lies and wondering what would be the fitting procedure.

Ten o'clock passed thus, and eleven. At twelve o'clock, when Asayo for the sixth or seventh time was assuring Ichibei that everything possible had been done for her blind husband, a wind storm suddenly arose, and in the midst of it was heard the sound of the *amma*'s flute, just as Yoichi played it; it was so unmistakably his that Asayo screamed with fear.

At first distant, nearer and nearer approached the sound, until at last it seemed to be in the room itself. At that moment a cold puff of air came down the *tem-mado* and the ghost of Yoichi was seen standing beneath it, a cold, white, glimmering and sad-faced wraith.

Tamataro and his wife tried to get up and run out of the house, but they found that their legs would not support them, so full were they of fear.

Tamataro seized a lamp and flung it at the ghost, but the ghost was not to be moved. The lamp passed through him and broke, setting fire to the house, which burned instantly, the wind fanning the flames.

Ichibei made his escape, but neither Asayo nor her husband could move, and the flames consumed them in the presence of Yoichi's ghost. Their cries were loud and piercing.

Ichibei had all the ashes swept up and placed in a tomb. He had buried in another grave the flute of the blind *amma*, and erected on the ground where the house had been a monument sacred to the memory of Yoichi.

It is known as *Fuezuka No Kwaidan* (The Flute Ghost Tomb).

R. G. S.
1908

Of a Promise Broken

I

'I am not afraid to die,' said the dying wife. 'There is only one thing that troubles me now. I wish that I could know who will take my place in this house.'

'My dear one,' answered the sorrowing husband, 'nobody shall ever take your place in my home. I will never, never marry again.'

At the time that he said this he was speaking out of his heart, for he loved the woman whom he was about to lose.

'On the faith of a samurai?' she questioned, with a feeble smile.

'On the faith of a samurai,' he responded, stroking the pale thin face.

'Then, my dear one,' she said, 'you will let me be buried in the garden, will you not? Near those plum trees that we planted at the further end? I wanted long ago to ask this, but I thought that if you were to marry again, you would not like to have my grave so near you. Now you have promised that no other woman shall take my place, so I need not hesitate to speak of my wish . . . I want so much to be buried in the garden! I think that in the garden I should sometimes hear your voice, and that I should still be able to see the flowers in the spring.'

'It shall be as you wish,' he answered. 'But do not now speak of burial: you are not so ill that we have lost all hope.'

'I have,' she returned. 'I shall die this morning . . . But you will bury me in the garden?'

'Yes,' he said, 'under the shade of the plum trees that we planted; and you shall have a beautiful tomb there.'

'And will you give me a little bell?'

'Bell – ?'

'Yes: I want you to put a little bell in the coffin – such a little bell as the Buddhist pilgrims carry. Shall I have it?'

'You shall have the little bell, and anything else that you wish.'

'I do not wish for anything else,' she said. 'My dear one, you have been very good to me always. Now I can die happy.'

Then she closed her eyes and died – as easily as a tired child falls asleep. She looked beautiful when she was dead, and there was a smile upon her face.

She was buried in the garden, under the shade of the trees that she loved; and a small bell was buried with her. Above the grave was erected a handsome monument, decorated with the family crest, and bearing the *kaimyô*: 'Great Elder Sister, Luminous-Shadow-of-the-Plum-Flower-Chamber, dwelling in the Mansion of the Great Sea of Compassion.'

But, within a twelve-month after the death of his wife, the relatives and friends of the samurai began to insist that he should marry again.

'You are still a young man,' they said, 'and an only son; and you have no children. It is the duty of a samurai to marry. If you die childless, who will there be to make the offerings and to remember the ancestors?'

By many such representations he was at last persuaded to

marry again. The bride was only seventeen years old; and he found that he could love her dearly, notwithstanding the dumb reproach of the tomb in the garden.

II

Nothing took place to disturb the happiness of the young wife until the seventh day after the wedding, when her husband was ordered to undertake certain duties requiring his presence at the castle by night. On the first evening that he was obliged to leave her alone, she felt uneasy in a way that she could not explain – vaguely afraid without knowing why. When she went to bed she could not sleep. There was a strange oppression in the air – an indefinable heaviness like that which sometimes precedes the coming of a storm. About the Hour of the Ox she heard, outside in the night, the clanging of a bell – a Buddhist pilgrim's bell – and she wondered what pilgrim could be passing through the samurai quarter at such a time. Presently, after a pause, the bell sounded much nearer. Evidently, the pilgrim was approaching the house – but why approaching from the rear, where no road was? . . . Suddenly, the dogs began to whine and howl in an unusual and horrible way – and a fear came upon her like the fear of dreams . . . That ringing was certainly in the garden . . . She tried to get up to waken a servant. But she found that she could not rise – could not move, could not call . . . And nearer and still more near came the clang of the bell – and oh! how the dogs howled! . . . Then, lightly as a shadow steals, there glided into the room a woman – though every door stood fast and every screen unmoved – a woman robed in a grave-robe and carrying a pilgrim's bell. Eyeless she came – because she had long been dead – and her loosened hair streamed down about her face – and she looked without eyes through the tangle of it and spoke without a tongue:

'Not in this house, not in this house shall you stay! Here I am mistress still. You shall go; and you shall tell to none the reason of your going. If you tell *him*, I will tear you into pieces!'

So speaking, the haunter vanished. The bride became senseless with fear. Until the dawn she so remained.

Nevertheless, in the cheery light of day, she doubted the reality of what she had seen and heard. The memory of the warning still weighed upon her so heavily that she did not dare to speak of the vision, either to her husband or to anyone else; but she was almost able to persuade herself that she had only dreamed an ugly dream, which had made her ill.

On the following night, however, she could not doubt. Again, at the Hour of the Ox, the dogs began to howl and whine – again the bell resounded, approaching slowly from the garden – again the listener vainly strove to rise and call – again the dead came into the room, and hissed:

'You shall go, and you shall tell to no one why you must go! If you even whisper it to *him* I will tear you in pieces!'

This time the haunter came close to the couch – and bent and muttered and moaned above it . . .

Next morning, when the samurai returned from the castle, his young wife prostrated herself before him in supplication:

'I beseech you,' she said, 'to pardon my ingratitude and my great rudeness in thus addressing you: but I want to go home – I want to go away at once.'

'Are you not happy here?' he asked, in sincere surprise. 'Has anyone dared to be unkind to you during my absence?'

'It is not that,' she answered, sobbing. 'Everybody here has been only too good to me . . . But I cannot continue to be your wife – I must go away.'

'My dear!' he exclaimed in great astonishment. 'It is very

painful to know that you have had any cause for unhappiness in this house. But I cannot even imagine why you should want to go away – unless somebody has been very unkind to you . . . Surely you do not mean that you wish for a divorce?'

She responded, trembling and weeping:

'If you do not give me a divorce, I shall die!'

He remained for a little while silent, vainly trying to think of some cause for this amazing declaration. Then, without betraying any emotion, he made answer:

'To send you back now to your people, without any fault on your part, would seem a shameful act. If you will tell me a good reason for your wish – any reason that will enable me to explain matters honourably – I can write you a divorce. But unless you give me a reason, a good reason, I will not divorce you – for the honour of our house must be kept above reproach.'

And then she felt obliged to speak, and she told him everything, adding, in an agony of terror:

'Now that I have let you know, she will kill me! – she will kill me!'

Although a brave man, and little inclined to believe in phantoms, the samurai was more than startled for the moment. But a simple and natural explanation of the matter soon presented itself to his mind.

'My dear,' he said, 'you are now very nervous, and I fear that someone has been telling you foolish stories. I cannot give you a divorce merely because you have had a bad dream in this house. But I am very sorry indeed that you should have been suffering in such a way during my absence. Tonight, also, I must be at the castle, but you shall not be alone. I will order two of the retainers to keep watch in your room and you will be able to sleep in peace. They are good men and they will take all possible care of you.'

Then he spoke to her so considerately and so affectionately

that she became almost ashamed of her terrors and resolved to remain in the house.

III

The two retainers left in charge of the young wife were big, brave, simple-hearted men – experienced guardians of women and children. They told the bride pleasant stories to keep her cheerful. She talked with them a long time, laughed at their good-humoured fun and almost forgot her fears. When at last she lay down to sleep, the men-at-arms took their places in a corner of the room, behind a screen, and began a game of go – speaking only in whispers, that she might not be disturbed. She slept like an infant.

But again at the Hour of the Ox she awoke with a moan of terror – for she heard the bell! . . . It was already near and was coming nearer. She started up; she screamed – but in the room there was no stir – only a silence as of death – a silence growing – a silence thickening. She rushed to the men-at-arms: they sat before their checker-table, motionless, each staring at the other with fixed eyes. She shrieked to them. She shook them. They remained as if frozen . . .

Afterwards they said that they had heard the bell – heard also the cry of the bride – even felt her try to shake them into wakefulness – and that, nevertheless, they had not been able to move or speak. From the same moment they had ceased to hear or to see: a black sleep had seized upon them.

Entering his bridal chamber at dawn, the samurai beheld, by the light of a dying lamp, the headless body of his young wife, lying in a pool of blood. Still squatting before their unfinished game, the two retainers slept. At their master's cry they sprang up and stupidly stared at the horror on the floor . . .

The head was nowhere to be seen – and the hideous wound showed that it had not been cut off, but torn off. A trail of blood led from the chamber to an angle of the outer gallery, where the storm doors appeared to have been riven apart. The three men followed that trail into the garden – over reaches of grass, over spaces of sand, along the bank of an iris-bordered pond, under heavy shadowings of cedar and bamboo. And suddenly, at a turn, they found themselves face to face with a nightmare-thing that chippered like a bat: the figure of the long-buried woman, erect before her tomb – in one hand clutching a bell, in the other the dripping head . . . For a moment the three stood numbed. Then one of the men-at-arms, uttering a Buddhist invocation, drew and struck at the shape. Instantly, it crumbled down upon the soil – an empty scattering of grave-rags, bones and hair – and the bell rolled clanking out of the ruin. But the fleshless right hand, though parted from the wrist, still writhed – and its fingers still gripped at the bleeding head – and tore and mangled – as the claws of the yellow crab cling fast to a fallen fruit . . .

*

('That is a wicked story,' I said to the friend who had related it. 'The vengeance of the dead – if taken at all – should have been taken upon the man.'

'Men think so,' he made answer. 'But that is not the way that a woman feels.'

He was right.)

L. H.
1904

Ghost of the Violet Well

In the wild Province of Yamato, or very near to its borders, is a beautiful mountain known as Yoshino. It is not only known for its abundance of cherry blossom in the spring, but it is also celebrated in relation to more than one bloody battle. In fact, Yoshino might be called the staging place of historical battles. Many say, when in Yoshino, 'We are walking on history, because Yoshino itself is history.' Near Yoshino mountain lies another, known as Tsubosaka, and between them is the Valley of Shimizutani, in which is the Violet Well.

At the approach of spring in this *tani* (hollow) the grass assumes a perfect emerald green, while moss grows luxuriantly over rocks and boulders. Towards the end of April great patches of deep-purple wild violets show up in the lower parts of the valley, while up the sides pink and scarlet azaleas grow in a manner which beggars description.

Some thirty years ago a beautiful girl of the age of seventeen, named Shingé, was wending her way up Shimizutani, accompanied by four servants. All were out for a picnic, and all, of course, were in search of wildflowers. O Shingé San was the daughter of a daimio who lived in the neighbourhood. Every year she was in the habit of having this picnic and coming to Shimizutani at the end of April to hunt for her favourite flower, the purple violet (*sumire*).

The five girls, carrying bamboo baskets, were eagerly collecting flowers, enjoying the occupation as only Japanese girls can. They raced in their rivalry to have the prettiest basketful. There not being so many purple violets as were wanted, O Shingé San said, 'Let us go to the northern end of the valley, where the Violet Well is.'

Naturally, the girls assented, and off they all ran, each eager to be there first, laughing as they went.

O Shingé outran the rest and arrived before any of them; and, espying a huge bunch of her favourite flowers, of the deepest purple and very sweet in smell, she flung herself down, anxious to pick them before the others came. As she stretched out her delicate hand to grasp them – oh, horror! – a great mountain snake raised his head from beneath his shady retreat. So frightened was O Shingé San, she fainted away on the spot.

In the meanwhile, the other girls had given up the race, thinking it would please their mistress to arrive first. They picked what they most fancied, chased butterflies and arrived fully fifteen minutes after O Shingé San had fainted.

On seeing her thus laid out on the grass, a great fear filled them that she was dead, and their alarm increased when they saw a large green snake coiled near her head.

They screamed, as do most girls amid such circumstances; but one of them, Matsu, who did not lose her head so much as the others, threw her basket of flowers at the snake, which, not liking the bombardment, uncoiled himself and slid away, hoping to find a quieter place. Then all four girls bent over their mistress. They rubbed her hands and threw water on her face, but without effect. O Shingé's beautiful complexion became paler and paler, while her red lips assumed the purplish hue that is a sign of approaching death. The girls were heartbroken. Tears coursed down their faces. They did not know what to do, for they could not carry her. What a terrible state of affairs!

Just at that moment they heard a man's voice close behind them:

'Do not be so sad! I can restore the young lady to consciousness if you will allow me.'

They turned and saw a remarkably handsome youth standing on the grass not ten feet away. He appeared as an angel from heaven.

Without saying more, the young man approached the prostrate figure of O Shingé and, taking her hand in his, felt her pulse. None of the servants liked to interfere in this breach of etiquette. He had not asked permission, but his manner was so gentle and sympathetic that they could say nothing.

The stranger examined O Shingé carefully, keeping silence. Having finished, he took out of his pocket a little case of medicine and, putting some white powder from this into a paper, said:

'I am a doctor from a neighbouring village, and I have just been to see a patient at the end of the valley. By good fortune I returned this way, and am able to help you and save your mistress's life. Give her this medicine, while I hunt for and kill the snake.'

O Matsu San forced the medicine, along with a little water, into her mistress's mouth, and in a few minutes she began to recover.

Shortly after this the doctor returned, carrying the dead snake on a stick.

'Is this the snake you saw lying by your young mistress?' he asked.

'Yes, yes,' they cried, 'that is the horrible thing.'

'Then,' said the doctor, 'it is lucky I came, for it is very poisonous, and I fear your mistress would soon have died had I not arrived and been able to give her the medicine. Ah! I see that it is already doing the beautiful young lady good.'

On hearing the young man's voice, O Shingé San sat up.

'Pray, sir, may I ask to whom I am indebted for bringing me thus back to life?' she asked.

The doctor did not answer, but in a proud and manly way contented himself by smiling and bowing low and respectfully after the Japanese fashion; and departed as quietly and unassumingly as he had arrived, disappearing in the sleepy mist which always appears in the afternoons of springtime in the Shimizu Valley.

The four girls helped their mistress home; but indeed she wanted little assistance, for the medicine had done her much good and she felt quite recovered. O Shingé's father and mother were very grateful for their daughter's recovery, but the name of the handsome young doctor remained a secret to all except the servant girl Matsu.

For four days O Shingé remained quite well, but on the fifth day, for some cause or another, she took to her bed, saying she was sick. She did not sleep and did not wish to talk, but only to think and think and think. Neither father nor mother could make out what her illness was. There was no fever.

Doctors were sent for, one after another, but none of them could say what was the matter. All they saw was that she daily became weaker. Asano Zembei, Shingé's father, was heartbroken, and so was his wife. They had tried everything and failed to do the slightest good to poor O Shingé.

One day O Matsu San craved an interview with Asano Zembei – who, by the by, was the head of all his family, a daimio and great grandee. Zembei was not accustomed to listen to servants' opinions, but, knowing that O Matsu was faithful to his daughter and loved her very nearly as much as he did himself, he consented to hear her, and O Matsu was ushered into his presence.

'Oh, master,' said the servant, 'if you will let me find a

doctor for my young mistress, I can promise to find one who will cure her.'

'Where on earth will you find such a doctor? Have we not had all the best doctors in the province and some even from the capital? Where do you propose to look for one?'

O Matsu answered:

'Ah, master, my mistress is not suffering from an illness which can be cured by medicines – not even if they be given by the quart. Nor are doctors of much use. There is, however, one that I know of who could cure her. My mistress's illness is of the heart. The doctor I know of can cure her. It is for love of him that her heart suffers; it has suffered so from the day when he saved her life from the snake bite.'

Then O Matsu told particulars of the adventure at the picnic which had not been told before – for O Shingé had asked her servants to say as little as possible, fearing they would not be allowed to go to the Valley of the Violet Well again.

'What is the name of this doctor?' asked Asano Zembei, 'and who is he?'

'Sir,' answered O Matsu, 'he is Doctor Yoshisawa, a very handsome young man of most courtly manners; but he is of low birth, being only of the *eta*.* Please think, master, of my young mistress's burning heart, full of love for the man who saved her life – and no wonder, for he is very handsome and has the manners of a proud samurai. The only cure for your daughter, sir, is to be allowed to marry her lover.'

O Shingé's mother felt very sad when she heard this. She knew well (perhaps by experience) of the illnesses caused by love. She wept and said to Zembei:

'I am quite with you in sorrow, my lord, at the terrible trouble

* The *eta* are the lowest people or caste in Japan – skinners and killers of animals.

that has come to us, but I cannot see my daughter die thus. Let us tell her we will make inquiries about the man she loves, and see if we can make him our son-in-law. In any case, it is the custom to make full inquiries, which will extend over some days; and in this time our daughter may recover somewhat and get strong enough to hear the news that we cannot accept her lover as our son-in-law.'

Zembei agreed to this, and O Matsu promised to say nothing to her mistress of the interview.

O Shingé San was told by her mother that her father, though he had not consented to the engagement, had promised to make inquiries about Yoshisawa.

O Shingé took food and regained much strength on this news; and when she was strong enough, some ten days later, she was called into her father's presence, accompanied by her mother.

'My sweet daughter,' said Zembei, 'I have made careful inquiries about Doctor Yoshisawa, your lover. Deeply as it grieves me to say so, it is impossible that I, your father, the head of our whole family, can consent to your marriage with one of so low a family as Yoshisawa, who, in spite of his own goodness, has sprung from the *eta*. I must hear no more of it. Such a contract would be impossible for the Asano family.'

No one ventured to say a word to this. In Japan the head of a family's decision is final.

Poor O Shingé bowed to her father and went to her own room, where she wept bitterly; O Matsu, the faithful servant, doing her best to console her.

Next morning, to the astonishment of the household, O Shingé San could nowhere be found. Search was made everywhere; even Doctor Yoshisawa joined in the search.

On the third day after the disappearance, one of the searchers looked down the Violet Well and saw poor O Shingé's floating body.

Two days later she was buried, and on that day Yoshisawa threw himself into the well.

The people say that even now, on wet, stormy nights, they see the ghost of O Shingé San floating over the well, while some declare that they hear the sound of a young man weeping in the Valley of Shimizutani.

R. G. S.
1908

Ikiryō ★

Formerly, in the quarter of Reiganjima in Tokyo, there was a great porcelain shop called the Setomonodana, kept by a rich man named Kihei. Kihei had in his employ, for many years, a head clerk named Rokubei. Under Rokubei's care the business prospered – and at last it grew so large that Rokubei found himself unable to manage it without help. He therefore asked and obtained permission to hire an experienced assistant; and he then engaged one of his own nephews – a young man about twenty-two years old, who had learned the porcelain trade in Osaka.

The nephew proved a very capable assistant – shrewder in business than his experienced uncle. His enterprise extended the trade of the house, and Kihei was greatly pleased. But about seven months after his engagement, the young man became very ill and seemed likely to die. The best physicians in Tokyo were summoned to attend him, but none of them could understand the nature of his sickness. They prescribed no medicine and expressed the opinion that such a sickness could only have been caused by some secret grief.

★ Literally, 'living spirit' – that is to say, the ghost of a person still alive. An *ikiryō* may detach itself from the body under the influence of anger, and proceed to haunt and torment the individual by whom the anger was caused.

Rokubei imagined that it might be a case of lovesickness. He therefore said to his nephew:

'I have been thinking that, as you are still very young, you might have formed some secret attachment which is making you unhappy – perhaps even making you ill. If this be the truth, you certainly ought to tell me all about your troubles. Here I stand to you in the place of a father, as you are far away from your parents; and if you have any anxiety or sorrow, I am ready to do for you whatever a father should do. If money can help you, do not be ashamed to tell me, even though the amount be large. I think that I could assist you; and I am sure that Kihei would be glad to do anything to make you happy and well.'

The sick youth appeared to be embarrassed by these kindly assurances; and for some little time he remained silent. At last he answered:

'Never in this world can I forget those generous words. But I have no secret attachment – no longing for any woman. This sickness of mine is not a sickness that doctors can cure; and money could not help me in the least. The truth is that I have been so persecuted in this house that I scarcely care to live. Everywhere – by day and by night, whether in the shop or in my room, whether alone or in company – I have been unceasingly followed and tormented by the Shadow of a woman. And it is long, long since I have been able to get even one night's rest. For as soon as I close my eyes, the Shadow of the woman takes me by the throat and strives to strangle me. So I cannot sleep . . .'

'And why did you not tell me this before?' asked Rokubei.

'Because I thought,' the nephew answered, 'that it would be of no use to tell you. The Shadow is not the ghost of a dead person. It is made by the hatred of a living person – a person whom you very well know.'

'What person?' questioned Rokubei, in great astonishment.

'The mistress of this house,' whispered the youth. 'The wife of Kihei Sama . . . She wishes to kill me.'

★

Rokubei was bewildered by this confession. He doubted nothing of what his nephew had said, but he could not imagine a reason for the haunting. An *ikiryō* might be caused by disappointed love or by violent hate – without the knowledge of the person from whom it had emanated. To suppose any love in this case was impossible – the wife of Kihei was considerably more than fifty years of age. But on the other hand, what could the young clerk have done to provoke hatred – a hatred capable of producing an *ikiryō*? He had been irreproachably well conducted, unfailingly courteous and earnestly devoted to his duties. The mystery troubled Rokubei; but, after careful reflection, he decided to tell everything to Kihei, and to request an investigation.

Kihei was astounded; but in the time of forty years he had never had the least reason to doubt the word of Rokubei. He therefore summoned his wife at once and carefully questioned her, telling her, at the same time, what the sick clerk had said. At first she turned pale and wept; but, after some hesitation, she answered frankly:

'I suppose that what the new clerk has said about the *ikiryō* is true – though I really tried never to betray, by word or look, the dislike which I could not help feeling for him. You know that he is very skilful in commerce – very shrewd in everything that he does. And you have given him much authority in this house – power over the apprentices and the servants. But our only son, who should inherit this business, is very simple-hearted and easily deceived; and I have long been thinking that your clever new clerk might so delude our boy as to get possession of all this property. Indeed, I am certain that your clerk could at any time, without the least difficulty and without the least risk to himself, ruin our business and ruin our son. And with this certainty in my mind, I cannot help fearing and hating the man. I have often and often wished that he were dead; I have even wished that it were in my own power to kill him . . . Yes, I know that it is wrong to hate any one in such a way; but I could not check the feeling. Night and day I have been wishing evil to that clerk. So I cannot doubt that he has really seen the thing of which he spoke to Rokubei.'

'How absurd of you,' exclaimed Kihei, 'to torment yourself thus! Up to the present time that clerk has done no single thing for which he could be blamed; and you have caused him to suffer cruelly . . . Now if I should send him away, with his uncle, to another town, to establish a branch business, could you not endeavour to think more kindly of him?'

'If I do not see his face or hear his voice,' the wife answered, 'if you will only send him away from this house – then I think that I shall be able to conquer my hatred of him.'

'Try to do so,' said Kihei, 'for, if you continue to hate him as you have been hating him, he will certainly die, and you will then be guilty of having caused the death of a man who has done us nothing but good. He has been, in every way, a most excellent servant.'

Then Kihei quickly made arrangements for the establishment of a branch house in another city; and he sent Rokubei there with the clerk, to take charge. And thereafter the *ikiryō* ceased to torment the young man, who soon recovered his health.

L. H.
1902

The Tongue-cut Sparrow

Long, long ago in Japan there lived an old man and his wife. The old man was a good, kind-hearted, hard-working old fellow, but his wife was a regular crosspatch, who spoiled the happiness of her home by her scolding tongue. She was always grumbling about something from morning to night. The old man had for a long time ceased to take any notice of her crossness. He was out most of the day at work in the fields, and as he had no child, for his amusement when he came home, he kept a tame sparrow. He loved the little bird just as much as if she had been his child.

When he came back at night after his hard day's work in the open air it was his only pleasure to pet the sparrow, to talk to her and to teach her little tricks, which she learned very quickly. The old man would open her cage and let her fly about the room, and they would play together. Then when supper-time came, he always saved some titbits from his meal with which to feed his little bird.

Now one day the old man went out to chop wood in the forest, and the old woman stopped at home to wash clothes. The day before, she had made some starch, and now when she came to look for it, it was all gone; the bowl which she had filled full yesterday was quite empty.

While she was wondering who could have used or stolen the

starch, down flew the pet sparrow, and, bowing her little feathered head – a trick which she had been taught by her master – the pretty bird chirped and said:

'It is I who have taken the starch. I thought it was some food put out for me in that basin and I ate it all. If I have made a mistake I beg you to forgive me! Tweet, tweet, tweet!'

You see from this that the sparrow was a truthful bird, and the old woman ought to have been willing to forgive her at once when she asked her pardon so nicely. But not so.

The old woman had never loved the sparrow, and had often quarrelled with her husband for keeping what she called a dirty bird about the house, saying that it only made extra work for her. Now she was only too delighted to have some cause of complaint against the pet. She scolded and even cursed the poor little bird for her bad behaviour, and, not content with using these harsh, unfeeling words, in a fit of rage she seized the sparrow – who all this time had spread out her wings and bowed her head before the old woman, to show how sorry she was – and fetched the scissors and cut off the poor little bird's tongue.

'I suppose you took my starch with that tongue! Now you may see what it is like to go without it!' And with these dreadful words she drove the bird away, not caring in the least what might happen to it and without the smallest pity for its suffering, so unkind was she!

The old woman, after she had driven the sparrow away, made some more rice paste, grumbling all the time at the trouble, and after starching all her clothes, spread the things on boards to dry in the sun, instead of ironing them as they do in England.

In the evening the old man came home. As usual, on the way back he looked forward to the time when he should reach his gate and see his pet come flying and chirping to meet him, ruffling out her feathers to show her joy, and at last coming to rest on his shoulder. But tonight the old man was very disappointed, for not even the shadow of his dear sparrow was to be seen.

He quickened his steps, hastily drew off his straw sandals and stepped on to the veranda. Still no sparrow was to be seen. He now felt sure that his wife, in one of her cross tempers, had shut the sparrow up in its cage. So he called her and said anxiously:

'Where is Suzume San (Miss Sparrow) today?'

The old woman pretended not to know at first, and answered:

'Your sparrow? I am sure I don't know. Now I come to think of it, I haven't seen her all the afternoon. I shouldn't wonder if the ungrateful bird had flown away and left you, after all your petting!'

But at last, when the old man gave her no peace, but asked her again and again, insisting that she must know what had happened to his pet, she confessed all. She told him crossly how the sparrow had eaten the rice paste she had specially made for starching her clothes, and how when the sparrow had confessed to what she had done, in great anger she had taken her scissors and cut out her tongue, and how finally she had driven the bird away and forbidden her to return to the house again.

Then the old woman showed her husband the sparrow's tongue, saying:

'Here is the tongue I cut off! Horrid little bird, why did it eat all my starch?'

'How could you be so cruel? Oh! how could you so cruel?' was all that the old man could answer. He was too kind-hearted to punish his shrew of a wife, but he was terribly distressed at what had happened to his poor little sparrow.

'What a dreadful misfortune for my poor Suzume San to lose her tongue!' he said to himself. 'She won't be able to chirp any more, and surely the pain of the cutting of it out in that rough way must have made her ill! Is there nothing to be done?'

The old man shed many tears after his cross wife had gone to sleep. While he wiped away the tears with the sleeve of his cotton robe, a bright thought comforted him: he would go and look for the sparrow on the morrow. Having decided this, he was able to go to sleep at last.

The next morning he rose early, as soon as ever the day broke, and, snatching a hasty breakfast, started out over the hills and through the woods, stopping at every clump of bamboos to cry:

'Where, oh where does my tongue-cut sparrow stay? Where, oh where, does my tongue-cut sparrow stay!'

He never stopped to rest for his noonday meal, and it was far on in the afternoon when he found himself near a large bamboo wood. Bamboo groves are the favourite haunts of sparrows, and there, sure enough, at the edge of the wood he saw his own dear sparrow waiting to welcome him. He could hardly believe his eyes for joy, and ran forward quickly to greet her. She bowed her little head and went through a number of the tricks her master had taught her, to show her pleasure at seeing her old friend again, and, wonderful to relate, she could talk as of old. The old man told her how sorry he was for all that had happened, and inquired after her tongue, wondering how she could speak so well without it. Then the sparrow opened her beak and showed him that a new tongue had grown in place of the old one, and begged him not to think any more about the past, for she was quite well now. Then the old man knew that his sparrow was a fairy and no common bird. It would be difficult to exaggerate the old man's rejoicing now. He forgot all his troubles, he forgot even how tired he was, for he had found his lost sparrow, and instead of being ill and without a tongue, as he had feared and expected to find her, she was well and happy and with a new tongue, and without a sign of the ill-treatment she had received from his wife. And above all she was a fairy.

The sparrow asked him to follow her, and, flying before him, she led him to a beautiful house in the heart of the bamboo grove. The old man was utterly astonished when he entered the house to find what a beautiful place it was. It was built of the whitest wood, the soft, cream-coloured mats which took the place of carpets were the finest he had ever seen, and the cushions that the sparrow brought out for him to sit on were made of the finest silk and crêpe. Beautiful vases and lacquer boxes adorned the *tokonoma*★ of every room.

The sparrow led the old man to the place of honour; and then, taking her place at a humble distance, she thanked him with many polite bows for all the kindness he had shown her for many long years.

Then the Lady Sparrow, as we will now call her, introduced all her family to the old man. This done, her daughters, robed in dainty crêpe gowns, brought in on beautiful old-fashioned trays a feast of all kinds of delicious foods, till the old man began to think he must be dreaming. In the middle of the dinner some of the sparrow's daughters performed a wonderful dance called the '*Suzume-Odori*' or 'Sparrow Dance' to amuse the guest.

Never had the old man enjoyed himself so much. The hours flew by too quickly in this lovely spot, with all these fairy sparrows to wait upon him and to feast him and to dance before him.

But the night came on and the darkness reminded him that he had a long way to go and must think about taking his leave and return home. He thanked his kind hostess for her splendid entertainment, and begged her for his sake to forget all she had suffered at the hands of his cross old wife. He told the Lady Sparrow that it was a great comfort and happiness to him to find her in such a beautiful home and to know that she wanted for nothing. It was his anxiety to know how she fared and what had really happened to her that had led him to seek her. Now he knew that all was well he could return home with a light heart.

★ An alcove where precious objects are displayed.

If ever she wanted him for anything she had only to send for him and he would come at once.

The Lady Sparrow begged him to stay and rest several days and enjoy the change, but the old man said he must return to his old wife – who would probably be cross at his not coming home at the usual time – and to his work, and therefore, much as he wished to do so, he could not accept her kind invitation. But now that he knew where the Lady Sparrow lived he would come to see her whenever he had the time.

When the Lady Sparrow saw that she could not persuade the old man to stay longer, she gave an order to some of her servants and they at once brought in two boxes, one large and the other small. These were placed before the old man, and the Lady Sparrow asked him to choose whichever he liked for a present, which she wished to give him.

The old man could not refuse this kind proposal, and he chose the smaller box, saying:

'I am now too old and feeble to carry the big and heavy box. As you are so kind as to say that I may take whichever I like, I will choose the small one, which will be easier for me to carry.'

Then the sparrows all helped him put it on his back and went to the gate to see him off, bidding him goodbye with many bows and entreating him to come again whenever he had the time. Thus the old man and his pet sparrow separated quite happily, the sparrow showing not the least ill will for all the unkindness she had suffered at the hands of the old wife. Indeed, she only felt sorrow for the old man who had to put up with it all his life.

When the old man reached home he found his wife even crosser than usual, for it was late on in the night and she had been waiting up for him for a long time.

'Where have you been all this time?' she asked in a big voice. 'Why do you come back so late?'

The old man tried to pacify her by showing her the box of

presents he had brought back with him, and then he told her of all that had happened to him and how wonderfully he had been entertained at the sparrow's house.

'Now let us see what is in the box,' said the old man, not giving her time to grumble again. 'You must help me open it.' And they both sat down before the box and opened it.

To their utter astonishment they found the box filled to the brim with gold and silver coins and many other precious things. The mats of their little cottage fairly glittered as they took out the things, one by one, and put them down and handled them over and over again. The old man was overjoyed at the sight of the riches that were now his. Beyond his brightest expectations was the sparrow's gift, which would enable him to give up work and live in ease and comfort the rest of his days.

He said: 'Thanks to my good little sparrow! Thanks to my good little sparrow!' many times.

But the old woman, after the first moments of surprise and satisfaction at the sight of the gold and silver were over, could not suppress the greed of her wicked nature. She now began to reproach the old man for not having brought home the big box of presents, for in the innocence of his heart he had told her how he had refused the large box of presents which the sparrows had offered him, preferring the smaller one because it was light and easy to carry home.

'You silly old man,' said she. 'Why did you not bring the large box? Just think what we have lost. We might have had twice as much silver and gold as this. You are certainly an old fool!' she screamed, and then went to bed as angry as she could be.

The old man now wished that he had said nothing about the big box, but it was too late; the greedy old woman, not contented with the good luck which had so unexpectedly befallen them and which she so little deserved, made up her mind, if possible, to get more.

Early the next morning she got up and made the old man describe the way to the sparrow's house. When he saw what was in her mind he tried to keep her from going, but it was useless. She would not listen to one word he said. It is strange that the old woman did not feel ashamed of going to see the sparrow after the cruel way she had treated her in cutting off her tongue in a fit of rage. But her greed to get the big box made her forget everything else. It did not even enter her thoughts that the sparrows might be angry with her – as, indeed, they were – and might punish her for what she had done.

Ever since the Lady Sparrow had returned home in the sad plight in which they had first found her, weeping and bleeding from the mouth, her whole family and relations had done little else but speak of the cruelty of the old woman.

'How could she,' they asked each other, 'inflict such a heavy punishment for such a trifling offence as that of eating some rice paste by mistake?'

They all loved the old man who was so kind and good and patient under all his troubles, but the old woman they hated, and they determined, if ever they had the chance, to punish her as she deserved. They had not long to wait.

After walking for some hours the old woman had at last found the bamboo grove which she had made her husband carefully describe, and now she stood before it crying out:

'Where is the tongue-cut sparrow's house? Where is the tongue-cut sparrow's house?'

At last she saw the eaves of the house peeping out from amongst the bamboo foliage. She hastened to the door and knocked loudly.

When the servants told the Lady Sparrow that her old mistress was at the door asking to see her, she was somewhat surprised at the unexpected visit, after all that had taken place, and she wondered not a little at the boldness of the old woman in venturing to come to the house. The Lady Sparrow, however, was a polite bird, and so she went out to greet the old woman, remembering that she had once been her mistress.

The old woman intended, however, to waste no time in words, she went right to the point, without the least shame, and said:

'You need not trouble to entertain me as you did my old man. I have come myself to get the box which he so stupidly left behind. I shall soon take my leave if you will give me the big box – that is all I want!'

The Lady Sparrow at once consented, and told her servants to bring out the big box. The old woman eagerly seized it and hoisted it on her back, and without even stopping to thank the Lady Sparrow began to hurry homewards.

The box was so heavy that she could not walk fast, much less run, as she would have liked to do, so anxious was she to get home and see what was inside the box, but she had often to sit down and rest herself by the way.

While she was staggering along under the heavy load, her desire to open the box became too great to be resisted. She could wait no longer, for she supposed this big box to be full of gold and silver and precious jewels like the small one her husband had received.

At last this greedy and selfish old woman put down the box by the wayside and opened it carefully, expecting to gloat her eyes on a mine of wealth. What she saw, however, so terrified her that she nearly lost her senses. As soon as she lifted the lid a number of horrible and frightful-looking demons bounced out of the box and surrounded her as if they intended to kill her. Not even in nightmares had she ever seen such horrible creatures as her much-coveted box contained. A demon with one huge eye right in the middle of its forehead came and glared at her, monsters with gaping mouths looked as if they would devour her, a huge snake coiled and hissed about her, and a big frog hopped and croaked towards her.

The old woman had never been so frightened in her life, and ran from the spot as fast as her quaking legs would carry her, glad to escape alive. When she reached home she fell to the floor and told her husband with tears all that had happened to her, and how she had been nearly killed by the demons in the box.

Then she began to blame the sparrow, but the old man stopped her at once, saying:

'Don't blame the sparrow. It is your wickedness which has at last met with its reward. I only hope this may be a lesson to you in the future!'

The old woman said nothing more, and from that day she repented of her cross, unkind ways, and by degrees became a good old woman, so that her husband hardly knew her to be the same person, and they spent their last days together happily, free from want or care, spending carefully the treasure the old man had received from his pet, the tongue-cut sparrow.

Y. T. O.
1903

The Dream of Akinosuké

In the district called Toichi of Yamato Province, there used to live a *gōshi* named Miyata Akinosuké . . . (Here I must tell you that in Japanese feudal times there was a privileged class of soldier-farmers — freeholders — corresponding to the class of yeomen in England; and these were called *gōshi*.)

In Akinosuké's garden there was a great and ancient cedar tree, under which he was wont to rest on sultry days. One very warm afternoon he was sitting under this tree with two of his friends, fellow-*gōshi*, chatting and drinking wine, when he felt all of a sudden very drowsy — so drowsy that he begged his friends to excuse him for taking a nap in their presence. Then he lay down at the foot of the tree and dreamed this dream:

He thought that as he was lying there in his garden, he saw a procession, like the train of some great daimio descending a hill nearby, and that he got up to look at it. A very grand procession it proved to be — more imposing than anything of the kind which he had ever seen before; and it was advancing towards his dwelling. He observed in the van of it a number of young men richly apparelled, who were drawing a great lacquered palace-carriage or *gosho-guruma*, hung with bright blue silk. When the procession arrived within a short distance of the house it halted; and a richly dressed man — evidently a person of rank — advanced

from it, approached Akinosuké, bowed to him profoundly, and
then said:

'Honoured sir, you see before you a *kérai* (vassal) of the *Kokuō*
of Tokoyo.* My master, the king, commands me to greet you in
his august name, and to place myself wholly at your disposal. He
also bids me inform you that he augustly desires your presence at
the palace. Be therefore pleased immediately to enter this honourable carriage, which he has sent for your conveyance.'

Upon hearing these words, Akinosuké wanted to make some
fitting reply; but he was too much astonished and embarrassed
for speech – and in the same moment his will seemed to melt
away from him, so that he could only do as the *kérai* bade him.
He entered the carriage; the *kérai* took a place beside him and
made a signal; the drawers, seizing the silken ropes, turned the
great vehicle southward – and the journey began.

In a very short time, to Akinosuké's amazement, the carriage
stopped in front of a huge, two-storeyed gateway (*rōmon*) of a
Chinese style, which he had never before seen. Here the *kérai*
dismounted, saying, 'I go to announce the honourable arrival' –
and he disappeared. After some little waiting, Akinosuké saw
two noble-looking men, wearing robes of purple silk and high
caps of the form indicating lofty rank, come from the gateway.
These, after having respectfully saluted him, helped him to
descend from the carriage, and led him through the great gate
and across a vast garden, to the entrance of a palace whose front
appeared to extend, west and east, to a distance of miles.
Akinosuké was then shown into a reception room of wonderful size and splendour. His guides conducted him to the place
of honour, and respectfully seated themselves apart; while
serving-maids, in costume of ceremony, brought refreshments.
When Akinosuké had partaken of the refreshments, the two

* 'King of Fairyland'.

purple-robed attendants bowed low before him and addressed him in the following words – each speaking alternately, according to the etiquette of courts:

'It is now our honourable duty to inform you . . . as to the reason of your having been summoned hither . . . Our master, the king, augustly desires that you become his son-in-law . . . and it is his wish and command that you shall wed this very day . . . the August Princess, his maiden-daughter . . . We shall soon conduct you to the presence chamber . . . where His Augustness even now is waiting to receive you . . . But it will be necessary that we first invest you . . . with the appropriate garments of ceremony.'

Having thus spoken, the attendants rose together and proceeded to an alcove containing a great chest of gold lacquer. They opened the chest and took from it various robes and girdles of rich material, and a *kamuri* or regal headdress. With these they attired Akinosuké as befitted a princely bridegroom; and he was then conducted to the presence room, where he saw the *Kokuō* of Tokoyo seated upon the *daiza* (dais), wearing a high black cap of state and robed in robes of yellow silk. Before the *daiza*, to left and right, a multitude of dignitaries sat in rank, as motionless and splendid as images in a temple; and Akinosuké, advancing into their midst, saluted the king with the triple prostration of usage. The king greeted him with gracious words, and then said:

'You have already been informed as to the reason of your having been summoned to our presence. We have decided that you shall become the adopted husband of our only daughter – and the wedding ceremony shall now be performed.'

As the king finished speaking, a sound of joyful music was heard; and a long train of beautiful court ladies advanced from behind a curtain to conduct Akinosuké to the room in which his bride awaited him.

The room was immense, but it could scarcely contain the multitude of guests assembled to witness the wedding ceremony. All bowed down before Akinosuké as he took his place, facing the king's daughter, on the kneeling-cushion prepared for him. As a maiden of heaven the bride appeared to be; and her robes were beautiful as a summer sky. And the marriage was performed amid great rejoicing.

Afterwards the pair were conducted to a suite of apartments that had been prepared for them in another portion of the palace; and there they received the congratulations of many noble persons, and wedding gifts beyond counting.

Some days later Akinosuké was again summoned to the throne room. On this occasion he was received even more graciously than before; and the king said to him:

'In the south-western part of our dominion there is an island called Raishū. We have now appointed you governor of that island. You will find the people loyal and docile, but their laws have not yet been brought into proper accord with the laws of Tokoyo, and their customs have not been properly regulated. We entrust you with the duty of improving their social condition as far as may be possible; and we desire that you shall rule them with kindness and wisdom. All preparations necessary for your journey to Raishū have already been made.'

So Akinosuké and his bride departed from the palace of Tokoyo, accompanied to the shore by a great escort of nobles and officials; and they embarked upon a ship of state provided by the king. And with favouring winds they safely sailed to Raishū, and found the good people of that island assembled upon the beach to welcome them.

Akinosuké entered at once upon his new duties; and they did not prove to be hard. During the first three years of his governorship he was occupied chiefly with the framing and the enactment of laws; but he had wise counsellors to help him, and he never found the work unpleasant. When it was all finished, he had no active duties to perform, beyond attending the rites and ceremonies ordained by ancient custom. The country was so healthy and so fertile that sickness and want were unknown; and the people were so good that no laws were ever broken. And Akinosuké dwelt and ruled in Raishū for twenty years more – making in all twenty-three years of sojourn, during which no shadow of sorrow traversed his life.

But in the twenty-fourth year of his governorship a great misfortune came upon him; for his wife, who had borne him seven children – five boys and two girls – fell sick and died. She was buried, with high pomp, on the summit of a beautiful hill in the district of Hanryōkō; and a monument, exceedingly splendid, was placed upon her grave. But Akinosuké felt such grief at her death that he no longer cared to live.

Now when the legal period of mourning was over, there came to Raishū, from the Tokoyo palace, a *shisha* or royal messenger. The *shisha* delivered to Akinosuké a message of condolence, and then said to him:

'These are the words which our august master, the King of Tokoyo, commands that I repeat to you: "We will now send you back to your own people and country. As for the seven children, they are the grandsons and granddaughters of the king, and shall be fitly cared for. Do not, therefore, allow your mind to be troubled concerning them."'

On receiving this mandate, Akinosuké submissively prepared for his departure. When all his affairs had been settled, and the ceremony of bidding farewell to his counsellors and trusted officials had been concluded, he was escorted with much honour to the port. There he embarked upon the ship sent for him; and the ship sailed out into the blue sea, under the blue sky; and the shape of the island of Raishū itself turned blue and then turned grey, and then vanished forever . . . And

Akinosuké suddenly awoke – under the cedar tree in his own garden!

For a moment he was stupefied and dazed. But he perceived his two friends still seated near him, drinking and chatting merrily. He stared at them in a bewildered way, and cried aloud:

'How strange!'

'Akinosuké must have been dreaming,' one of them exclaimed, with a laugh. 'What did you see, Akinosuké, that was strange?'

Then Akinosuké told his dream – that dream of three-and-twenty years' sojourn in the realm of Tokoyo, on the island of Raishū – and they were astonished, because he had really slept for no more than a few minutes.

One *gōshi* said:

'Indeed, you saw strange things. We also saw something strange while you were napping. A little yellow butterfly was fluttering over your face for a moment or two, and we watched it. Then it alighted on the ground beside you, close to the tree; and almost as soon as it alighted there, a big, big ant came out of a hole and seized it and pulled it down into the hole. Just before you woke up, we saw that very butterfly come out of the hole again and flutter over your face as before. And then it suddenly disappeared: we do not know where it went.'

'Perhaps it was Akinosuké's soul,' the other *gōshi* said. 'Certainly, I thought I saw it fly into his mouth . . . But, even if that butterfly *was* Akinosuké's soul, the fact would not explain his dream.'

'The ants might explain it,' returned the first speaker. 'Ants are queer beings – possibly goblins . . . Anyhow, there is a big ants' nest under that cedar tree.'

'Let us look!' cried Akinosuké, greatly moved by this suggestion. And he went for a spade.

The ground about and beneath the cedar tree proved to have

been excavated in a most surprising way by a prodigious colony of ants. The ants had furthermore built inside their excavations; and their tiny constructions of straw, clay and stems bore an odd resemblance to miniature towns. In the middle of a structure considerably larger than the rest there was a marvellous swarming of small ants around the body of one very big ant, which had yellowish wings and a long black head.

'Why, there is the king of my dream!' cried Akinosuké, 'and there is the palace of Tokoyo! . . . How extraordinary! . . . Raishū ought to lie somewhere south-west of it – to the left of that big root . . . Yes! – here it is! . . . How very strange! Now I am sure that I can find the mountain of Hanryōkō and the grave of the princess.'

In the wreck of the nest he searched and searched, and at last discovered a tiny mound, on the top of which was fixed a water-worn pebble, in shape resembling a Buddhist monument. Underneath it he found – embedded in clay – the dead body of a female ant.

L. H.
1904

The Eater of Dreams

Mijika-yo ya!
Baku no yumé kū
Hima mo nashi!

'Alas! how short this night of ours!
The *Baku* will not even have time to eat our dreams!'
– Old Japanese Love Song

The name of the creature is *Baku* or *Shirokinakatsukami*, and its particular function is the eating of dreams. It is variously represented and described. An ancient book in my possession states that the male *Baku* has the body of a horse, the face of a lion, the trunk and tusks of an elephant, the forelock of a rhinoceros, the tail of a cow, and the feet of a tiger. The female *Baku* is said to differ greatly in shape from the male, but the difference is not clearly set forth. In the time of the old Chinese learning, pictures of the *Baku* used to be hung up in Japanese houses, such pictures being supposed to exert the same beneficent power as the creature itself. My ancient book contains this legend about the custom:

'In the *Shōsei-Roku* it is declared that Kōtei, while hunting on the eastern coast, once met with a *Baku* having the body of an animal, but speaking like a man. Kōtei said: "Since the world is quiet and at peace, why should we still see goblins? If a *Baku* be needed to extinguish evil sprites, then it were better to have a picture of the *Baku* suspended to the wall of one's house. Thereafter, even though some evil wonder should appear, it could do no harm."'

Then there is given a long list of evil wonders and the signs of their presence:

'When the hen lays a soft egg, the demon's name is Taifu.

'When snakes appear entwined together, the demon's name is Jinzu.

'When dogs go with their ears turned back, the demon's name is Taiyō.

'When the fox speaks with the voice of a man, the demon's name is Gwaishū.

'When blood appears on the clothes of men, the demon's name is Yūki.

'When the rice pot speaks with a human voice, the demon's name is Kanjo.

'When the dream of the night is an evil dream, the demon's name is Ringetsu . . .'

And the old book further observes: 'Whenever any such evil marvel happens, let the name of the *Baku* be invoked: then the evil sprite will immediately sink three feet under the ground.'

*

But on the subject of evil wonders I do not feel qualified to discourse: it belongs to the unexplored and appalling world of Chinese demonology, and it has really very little to do with the subject of the *Baku* in Japan. The Japanese *Baku* is commonly known only as the Eater of Dreams; and the most remarkable fact in relation to the cult of the creature is that the Chinese character representing its name used to be put in gold upon the lacquered wooden pillows of lords and princes. By the virtue and power of this character on the pillow, the sleeper was thought to be protected from evil dreams. It is rather difficult to find such a pillow today: even pictures of the *Baku* (or *Hakutaku*, as it is sometimes called) have become very rare. But the old invocation to the *Baku* still survives in common parlance: *Baku kuraë! Baku kuraë!* – 'Devour, O *Baku!* devour my evil dream!' . . . When you awake from a nightmare or from any unlucky dream, you should quickly repeat that invocation three times – then the *Baku* will eat the dream, and will change the misfortune or the fear into good fortune and gladness.

*

It was on a very sultry night, during the Period of Greatest Heat, that I last saw the *Baku*. I had just awakened out of misery and the hour was the Hour of the Ox; and the *Baku* came in through the window to ask, 'Have you anything for me to eat?'

I gratefully made answer:

'Assuredly! . . . Listen, good *Baku*, to this dream of mine! –

'I was standing in some great white-walled room, where lamps were burning; but I cast no shadow on the naked floor of that room – and there, upon an iron bed, I saw my own dead body. How I had come to die, and when I had died, I could not remember. Women were sitting near the bed – six or seven – and I did not know any of them. They were neither young nor old, and all were dressed in black: watchers, I took them to be. They sat motionless and silent: there was no sound in the place; and I somehow felt that the hour was late.

'In the same moment I became aware of something nameless in the atmosphere of the room – a heaviness that weighed upon the will – some viewless, numbing power that was slowly growing. Then the watchers began to watch each other, stealthily;

and I knew that they were afraid. Soundlessly, one rose up and left the room. Another followed, then another. So, one by one, and as lightly as shadows, they all went out. I was left alone with the corpse of myself.

'The lamps still burned clearly, but the terror in the air was thickening. The watchers had stolen away almost as soon as they began to feel it. But I believed that there was yet time to escape – I thought that I could safely delay a moment longer. A monstrous curiosity obliged me to remain: I wanted to look at my own body, to examine it closely . . . I approached it. I observed it. And I wondered – because it seemed to me very long – unnaturally long . . .

'Then I thought that I saw one eyelid quiver. But the appearance of motion might have been caused by the trembling of a lamp flame. I stooped to look – slowly and very cautiously, because I was afraid that the eyes might open.

' "It is myself," I thought, as I bent down, "and yet, it is growing queer!" . . . The face appeared to be lengthening . . . "It is not myself," I thought again, as I stooped still lower, "and yet, it cannot be any other!" And I became much more afraid, unspeakably afraid, that the eyes would open . . .

'*They opened!* – horribly they opened! – and that thing sprang – sprang from the bed at me and fastened upon me – moaning and gnawing and rending! Oh! with what madness of terror did I strive against it! But the eyes of it, and the moans of it, and the touch of it, sickened; and all my being seemed about to burst asunder in a frenzy of loathing, when – I knew not how –

'I found in my hand an axe. And I struck with the axe – I clove, I crushed, I brayed the moaner – until there lay before me only a shapeless, hideous, reeking mass – the abominable ruin of myself . . .

'*Baku kuraë! Baku kuraë! Baku kuraë!* Devour, O *Baku!* Devour the dream!'

'Nay!' made answer the *Baku.* 'I never eat lucky dreams. That is a very lucky dream – a most fortunate dream . . . The axe – yes! The Axe of the Excellent Law, by which the monster of Self is utterly destroyed! . . . The best kind of a dream! My friend, *I* believe in the teaching of the Buddha.'

And the *Baku* went out of the window. I looked after him – and I beheld him fleeing over the miles of moonlit roofs – passing, from housetop to housetop, with amazing soundless leaps – like a great cat . . .

L. H.
1902

The Secret of Iidamachi Pond

In the first year of Bunkiu (1861–1864) there lived a man called Yehara Keisuke in Kasumigaseki, in the district of Kojimachi. He was a *hatomoto* – that is, a feudatory vassal of the Shogun – and a man to whom some respect was due; but apart from that, Yehara was much liked for his kindness of heart and general fairness in dealing with people. In Iidamachi lived another *hatomoto*, Hayashi Hayato. He had been married to Yehara's sister for five years. They were exceedingly happy; their daughter, four years old now, was the delight of their hearts. Their cottage was rather dilapidated, but it was Hayashi's own, with the pond in front of it, and two farms, the whole property comprising some 200 acres, of which nearly half was under cultivation. Thus Hayashi was able to live without working much. In the summer he fished for carp; in the winter he wrote much and was considered a bit of a poet.

At the time of this story, Hayashi, having planted his rice and *sato-imo* (sweet potatoes), had but little to do, and spent most of his time with his wife, fishing in his ponds, one of which contained large *suppon* (terrapin turtles) as well as koi (carp). Suddenly things went wrong.

Yehara was surprised one morning to receive a visit from his sister O Komé.

'I have come, dear brother,' she said, 'to beg you to help me to obtain a divorce or separation from my husband.'

'Divorce! Why should you want a divorce? Have you not always said you were happy with your husband, my dear friend Hayashi? For what sudden reason do you ask for a divorce? Remember you have been married for five years now, and that is sufficient to prove that your life has been happy, and that Hayashi has treated you well.'

At first O Komé would not give any reason why she wished to be separated from her husband; but at last she said:

'Brother, think not that Hayashi has been unkind. He is all that can be called kind, and we deeply love each other; but, as you know, Hayashi's family have owned the land, the farms on one of which latter we live, for some 300 years. Nothing would induce him to change his place of abode, and I should never have wished him to do so until some twelve days ago.'

'What has happened within these twelve wonderful days?' asked Yehara.

'Dear brother, I can stand it no longer,' was his sister's answer. 'Up to twelve days ago all went well; but then a terrible thing happened. It was very dark and warm, and I was sitting outside our house looking at the clouds passing over the moon, and talking to my daughter. Suddenly there appeared, as if walking on the lilies of the pond, a white figure. Oh, so white, so wet, and so miserable to look at! It appeared to arise from the pond and float in the air, and then approached me slowly until it was within ten feet. As it came, my child cried: "Why, Mother, there comes O Sumi – do you know O Sumi?" I answered her that I did not, I think; but in truth I was so frightened I hardly know what I said. The figure was horrible to look at. It was that of a girl of eighteen or nineteen years, with hair dishevelled and hanging loose, over white and wet shoulders. "Help me! Help me!" cried the figure, and I was so frightened that I covered my eyes and screamed for my husband, who was inside. He came out and found me in a dead faint, with my child by my side, also in a state of terror. Hayashi had seen nothing. He carried us both in, shut the doors, and told me I must have been dreaming. "Perhaps," he sarcastically added, "you saw the *kappa* (a mythical beast, half-turtle, half-man) which is said to dwell in the pond, but which none of my family have seen for over one hundred years." That is all that my husband said on the subject. Next night, however, when in bed, my child seized me suddenly, crying in terror-stricken tones, "O Sumi – here is O Sumi – how horrible she looks! Mother, Mother, do you see her?" I did see her. She stood dripping wet within three feet of my bed, the whiteness and the wetness and the dishevelled hair being what gave her the awful look which she bore. "Help me! Help me!" cried the figure, and then disappeared. After that I could not sleep; nor could I get my child to do so. On every night until now the ghost has come – O Sumi, as my child calls her. I should kill myself if I had to remain longer in that house, which has become a terror to myself and my child. My husband does not see the ghost and only laughs at me; and that is why I see no way out of the difficulty but a separation.'

Yehara told his sister that on the following day he would call on Hayashi, and sent his sister back to her husband that night.

Next day, when Yehara called, Hayashi, after hearing what the visitor had to say, answered:

'It is very strange. I was born in this house over twenty years ago; but I have never seen the ghost which my wife refers to, and have never heard about it. Not the slightest allusion to it was ever made by my father or mother. I will make inquiries of all my neighbours and servants, and ascertain if they ever heard of the ghost, or even of anyone coming to a sudden and untimely end. There must be something: it is impossible that my little child should know the name Sumi, she never having known anyone bearing it.'

Inquiries were made, but nothing could be learned from the servants or from the neighbours. Hayashi reasoned that, the ghost being always wet, the mystery might be solved by drying up the pond – perhaps to find the remains of some murdered person, whose bones required decent burial and prayers said over them.

The pond was old and deep, covered with water plants, and had never been emptied within his memory. It was said to contain a *kappa*. In any case, there were many terrapin turtles, the capture of which would well repay the cost of the emptying.

The bank of the pond was cut, and next day there remained only a pool in the deepest part; Hayashi decided to clear even this and dig into the mud below.

At this moment the grandmother of Hayashi arrived, an old woman of some eighty years, and said:

'You need go no farther. I can tell you all about the ghost. O Sumi does not rest, and it is quite true that her ghost appears. I am very sorry about it, now in my old age; for it is my fault – the sin is mine. Listen and I will tell you all.'

Everyone stood astonished at these words, feeling that some secret was about to be revealed.

The old woman continued:

'When Hayashi Hayato, your grandfather, was alive, we had a beautiful servant girl, seventeen years of age, called O Sumi. Your grandfather became enamoured of this girl and she of him. I was about thirty at that time and was jealous, for my better looks had passed away. One day, when your grandfather was out, I took Sumi to the pond and gave her a severe beating. During the struggle she fell into the water and got entangled in the weeds; and there I left her, fully believing the water to be shallow and that she could get out. She did not succeed and was drowned. Your grandfather found her dead on his return. In those days the police were not very particular with their inquiries. The girl was buried, but nothing was said to me, and the matter soon blew over. Fourteen days ago was the fiftieth anniversary of this tragedy. Perhaps that is the reason of Sumi's ghost appearing; for appear she must, or your child could not have known of her name. It must be as your child says, and that the first time she appeared Sumi communicated her name.'

The old woman was shaking with fear, and advised them all to say prayers at O Sumi's tomb. This was done, and the ghost has been seen no more. Hayashi said:

'Though I am a samurai and have read many books, I never believed in ghosts, but now I do.'

R. G. S.
1908

The Legend of Yurei-Daki

Near the village of Kurosaka, in the Province of Hōki, there is a waterfall called Yurei-Daki or The Cascade of Ghosts. Why it is so called I do not know. Near the foot of the fall there is a small Shintō shrine of the god of the locality, whom the people name Taki-Daimyōjin; and in front of the shrine is a little wooden money-box (*saisen-bako*) to receive the offerings of believers. And there is a story about that money-box.

One icy winter's evening, thirty-five years ago, the women and girls employed at a certain *asa-toriba* or hemp factory in Kurosaka, gathered around the big brazier in the spinning-room after their day's work had been done. Then they amused themselves by telling ghost stories. By the time that a dozen stories had been told, most of the gathering felt uncomfortable; and a girl cried out, just to heighten the pleasure of fear, 'Only think of going this night, all by one's self, to the Yurei-Daki!' The suggestion provoked a general scream, followed by nervous bursts of laughter . . .

'I'll give all the hemp I spun today,' mockingly said one of the party, 'to the person who goes!'

'So will I,' exclaimed another.

'And I,' said a third.

'All of us,' affirmed a fourth . . .

Then from among the spinners stood up one Yasumoto O-Katsu, the wife of a carpenter — she had her only son, a boy of two years old, snugly wrapped up and asleep upon her back.

'Listen,' said O-Katsu, 'if you will all really agree to make over to me all the hemp spun today, I will go to the Yurei-Daki.'

Her proposal was received with cries of astonishment and of defiance. But after having been several times repeated, it was seriously taken. Each of the spinners in turn agreed to give up her share of the day's work to O-Katsu, providing that O-Katsu should go to the Yurei-Daki.

'But how are we to know if she really goes there?' a sharp voice asked.

'Why, let her bring back the money-box of the god,' answered an old woman whom the spinners called Obaa San, the Grand-mother, 'that will be proof enough.'

'I'll bring it,' cried O-Katsu.

And out she darted into the street, with her sleeping boy upon her back.

*

The night was frosty, but clear. Down the empty street O-Katsu hurried; and she saw that all the house fronts were tightly closed, because of the piercing cold. Out of the village and along the high road she ran — *pichà-pichà* — with the great silence of frozen rice fields on either hand, and only the stars to light her. Half an hour she followed the open road; then she turned down a narrower way, winding under cliffs. Darker and rougher the path became as she proceeded; but she knew it well and she soon heard the dull roar of the water. A few minutes more and the way widened into a glen — and the dull roar suddenly became a loud clamour — and before her she saw, looming against a mass of blackness, the long glimmering of the fall. Dimly she perceived the shrine — the money-box. She rushed forward — put out her hand . . .

'*Oi!* O-Katsu San!' suddenly called a warning voice above the crash of the water.

O-Katsu stood motionless, stupefied by terror.

'*Oi!* O-Katsu San!' again pealed the voice – this time with more of menace in its tone.

But O-Katsu was really a bold woman. At once recovering from her stupefaction, she snatched up the money-box and ran. She neither heard nor saw anything more to alarm her until she reached the high road, where she stopped a moment to take breath. Then she ran on steadily – *pichà-pichà* – till she got to Kurosaka and thumped at the door of the *asa-toriba*.

*

How the women and the girls cried out as she entered, panting, with the money-box of the god in her hand! Breathlessly, they heard her story; sympathetically, they screeched when she told them of the voice that had called her name, twice, out of the haunted water . . . What a woman! Brave O-Katsu! – Well had she earned the hemp! . . .

'But your boy must be cold, O-Katsu!' cried the Obaa San. 'Let us have him here by the fire!'

'He ought to be hungry,' exclaimed the mother. 'I must give him his milk presently.' . . .

'Poor O-Katsu!' said the Obaa San, helping to remove the wraps in which the boy had been carried. 'Why, you are all wet behind!' Then, with a husky scream, the helper vociferated, '*Arà! It is blood!*'

And out of the wrappings unfastened there fell to the floor a blood-soaked bundle of baby clothes that left exposed two very small brown feet, and two very small brown hands – nothing more. The child's head had been torn off! . . .

L. H.
1902

Yuki Onna

In a village of Musashi Province, there lived two woodcutters: Mosaku and Minokichi. At the time of which I am speaking, Mosaku was an old man; and Minokichi, his apprentice, was a lad of eighteen years. Every day they went together to a forest situated about five miles from their village. On the way to that forest there is a wide river to cross; and there is a ferry boat. Several times a bridge was built where the ferry is, but the bridge was each time carried away by a flood. No common bridge can resist the current there when the river rises.

Mosaku and Minokichi were on their way home one very cold evening when a great snowstorm overtook them. They reached the ferry and they found that the boatman had gone away, leaving his boat on the other side of the river. It was no day for swimming; and the woodcutters took shelter in the ferryman's hut, thinking themselves lucky to find any shelter at all. There was no brazier in the hut, nor any place in which to make a fire: it was only a two-mat hut with a single door, but no window. Mosaku and Minokichi fastened the door and lay down to rest, with their straw raincoats over them. At first they did not feel very cold, and they thought that the storm would soon be over.

The old man almost immediately fell asleep; but the boy,

Minokichi, lay awake a long time, listening to the awful wind and the continual slashing of the snow against the door. The river was roaring; and the hut swayed and creaked like a junk at sea. It was a terrible storm; and the air was every moment becoming colder; and Minokichi shivered under his raincoat. But at last, in spite of the cold, he too fell asleep.

He was awakened by a showering of snow in his face. The door of the hut had been forced open; and, by the snow-light (*yuki-akari*), he saw a woman in the room – a woman all in white. She was bending above Mosaku and blowing her breath upon him – and her breath was like a bright white smoke. Almost in the same moment she turned to Minokichi and stooped over him. He tried to cry out, but found that he could not utter any sound. The white woman bent down over him, lower and lower, until her face almost touched him; and he saw that she was very beautiful – though her eyes made him afraid. For a little time she continued to look at him; then she smiled and she whispered:

'I intended to treat you like the other man. But I cannot help feeling some pity for you, because you are so young . . . You are a pretty boy, Minokichi, and I will not hurt you now. But if you ever tell anybody – even your own mother – about what you have seen this night, I shall know it, and then I will kill you . . . Remember what I say!'

With these words, she turned from him and passed through the doorway. Then he found himself able to move; and he sprang up and looked out. But the woman was nowhere to be seen, and the snow was driving furiously into the hut. Minokichi closed the door and secured it by fixing several billets of wood against it. He wondered if the wind had blown it open – he thought that he might have been only dreaming and might have mistaken the gleam of the snow-light in the doorway for the figure of a white woman: but he could not be sure. He called to Mosaku, and was frightened because the old man did not answer. He put out his hand in the dark and touched Mosaku's face, and found that it was ice! Mosaku was stark and dead . . .

By dawn the storm was over; and when the ferryman returned to his station, a little after sunrise, he found Minokichi lying senseless beside the frozen body of Mosaku. Minokichi was promptly cared for, and soon came to himself; but he remained a long time ill from the effects of the cold of that terrible night. He had been greatly frightened also by the old man's death; but he said nothing about the vision of the woman in white. As soon as he got well again, he returned to his calling, going alone every morning to the forest and coming back at nightfall with his bundles of wood, which his mother helped him to sell.

One evening, in the winter of the following year, as he was on his way home, he overtook a girl who happened to be travelling by the same road. She was a tall, slim girl, very good-looking, and she answered Minokichi's greeting in a voice as pleasant to the ear as the voice of a songbird. Then he walked beside her and they began to talk. The girl said that her name was O-Yuki (Snow); that she had lately lost both of her parents; and that she was going to Tokyo, where she happened to have some poor relations, who might help her to find a situation as servant. Minokichi soon felt charmed by this strange girl; and the more that he looked at her, the handsomer she appeared to be. He asked her whether she was yet betrothed, and she answered, laughingly, that she was free. Then, in her turn, she asked Minokichi whether he was married or pledged to marry; and he told her that, although he had only a widowed mother to support, the question of an 'honourable daughter-in-law' had not yet been considered, as he was very young . . . After these confidences, they walked on for a long while without speaking; but, as the proverb declares, '*Ki ga aréba, mé mo kuchi hodo ni mono wo iu*': 'When the wish is there, the eyes can say as much as the mouth.' By the time they reached the village, they had become very much pleased with each other; and then Minokichi asked O-Yuki to rest awhile at his house. After some shy hesitation, she went there with him; and his mother made her welcome and prepared a warm meal for her. O-Yuki behaved so nicely that Minokichi's mother took a sudden fancy to her, and persuaded her to delay her journey to Tokyo. And the natural end of the matter was that Yuki never went to Tokyo at all. She remained in the house as an 'honourable daughter-in-law'.

O-Yuki proved a very good daughter-in-law. When Minokichi's mother came to die – some five years later – her last words were words of affection and praise for the wife of her son. And O-Yuki bore Minokichi ten children, boys and girls – handsome children all of them and very fair of skin.

The country folk thought O-Yuki a wonderful person, by nature different from themselves. Most of the peasant women age early, but O-Yuki, even after having become the mother of ten children, looked as young and fresh as on the day when she had first come to the village.

One night, after the children had gone to sleep, O-Yuki was sewing by the light of a paper lamp; and Minokichi, watching her, said:

'To see you sewing there, with the light on your face, makes me think of a strange thing that happened when I was a lad of eighteen. I then saw somebody as beautiful and white as you are now – indeed, she was very like you.'

Without lifting her eyes from her work, O-Yuki responded:

'Tell me about her . . . Where did you see her?'

Then Minokichi told her about the terrible night in the ferryman's hut – and about the White Woman that had stooped over him, smiling and whispering – and about the silent death of old Mosaku. And he said:

'Asleep or awake, that was the only time that I saw a being as beautiful as you. Of course, she was not a human being; and I was afraid of her – very much afraid – but she was so white I . . . Indeed, I have never been sure whether it was a dream that I saw or the Woman of the Snow.'

O-Yuki flung down her sewing, and arose and bowed above Minokichi where he sat, and shrieked into his face:

'It was I – I – I! Yuki it was! And I told you then that I would kill you if you ever said one word about it! . . . But for those children asleep there, I would kill you this moment! And now you had better take very, very good care of them; for if ever they have reason to complain of you, I will treat you as you deserve!'

Even as she screamed, her voice became thin, like a crying of wind – then she melted into a bright white mist that spired to the roof beams and shuddered away through the smoke-hole . . . Never again was she seen.

L. H.
1904

The Snow Ghost

Perhaps there are not many, even in Japan, who have heard of the *Yuki Onna* (Snow Ghost). It is little spoken of except in the higher mountains, which are continually snow-clad in the winter. Those who have read Lafcadio Hearn's books will remember a story of the *Yuki Onna*, made much of on account of its beautiful telling, but in reality not better than the following.

Up in the northern Province of Echigo, opposite Sado Island on the Japan Sea, snow falls heavily. Sometimes there is as much as twenty feet of it on the ground, and many are the people who have been buried in the snows and never found until the spring. Not many years ago, three companies of soldiers, with the exception of three or four men, were destroyed in Aowomori; and it was many weeks before they were dug out – dead, of course.

Mysterious disappearances naturally give rise to fancies in a fanciful people, and from time immemorial the Snow Ghost has been one with the people of the north; while those of the south say that those of the north take so much sake that they see snow-covered trees as women.

Be that as it may, I must explain what a farmer called Kyuzae-mon saw.

In the village of Hoi, which consisted only of eleven houses, very poor ones at that, lived Kyuzaemon. He was poor and doubly unfortunate in having lost both his son and his wife. He led a lonely life.

In the afternoon of the 19th of January of the third year of Tem-po – that is, 1833 – a tremendous snowstorm came on. Kyuzaemon closed the shutters and made himself as comfortable as he could. Towards eleven o'clock at night he was awakened by a rapping at his door; it was a peculiar rap and came at regular intervals. Kyuzaemon sat up in bed, looked towards the door, and did not know what to think of this. The rapping came again, and with it the gentle voice of a girl. Thinking that it might be one of his neighbour's children wanting help, Kyuzaemon jumped out of bed; but when he got to the door he feared to open it. Voice and rapping coming again just as he reached it, he sprang back with a cry:

'Who are you? What do you want?'

'Open the door! Open the door!' came the voice from outside.

'Open the door! Is that likely until I know who you are and what you are doing out so late and on such a night?'

'But you must let me in. How can I proceed farther in this deep snow? I do not ask for food, but only for shelter.'

'I am very sorry, but I have no quilts or bedding. I can't possibly let you stay in my house.'

'I don't want quilts or bedding – only shelter,' pleaded the voice.

'I can't let you in, anyway,' shouted Kyuzaemon. 'It is too late and against the rules and the law.'

Saying which, Kyuzaemon re-barred his door with a strong piece of wood, never once having ventured to open a crack in the shutters to see who his visitor might be. As he turned towards his bed, with a shudder he beheld the figure of a woman standing beside it, clad in white, with her hair down her back.

She had not the appearance of a ghost; her face was pretty and she seemed to be about twenty-five years of age. Kyuzaemon, taken by surprise and very much alarmed, called out:

'Who and what are you, and how did you get in? Where did you leave your *geta*? (clogs)'

'I can come in anywhere when I choose,' said the figure, 'and I am the woman you would not let in. I require no clogs, for I whirl along over the snow, sometimes even flying through the air. I am on my way to visit the next village, but the wind is against me. That is why I wanted you to let me rest here. If you will do so, I shall start as soon as the wind goes down; in any case, I shall be gone by the morning.'

'I should not so much mind letting you rest if you were an ordinary woman. I should, in fact, be glad; but I fear spirits greatly, as my forefathers have done,' said Kyuzaemon.

'Be not afraid. You have a *butsudan* (family altar)?' said the figure.

'Yes, I have a *butsudan*,' said Kyuzaemon, 'but what can you want to do with that?'

'You say you are afraid of the spirits, of the effect that I may have upon you. I wish to pay my respects to your ancestors' tablets and assure their spirits that no ill shall befall you through me. Will you open and light the *butsudan*?'

'Yes,' said Kyuzaemon, with fear and trembling, 'I will open the *butsudan* and light the lamp. Please pray for me as well, for I am an unfortunate and unlucky man; but you must tell me in return who and what spirit you are.'

'You want to know much, but I will tell you,' said the spirit. 'I believe you are a good man. My name was Oyasu. I am the daughter of Yazaemon, who lives in the next village. My father, as perhaps you may have heard, is a farmer, and he adopted into his family, and as a husband for his daughter, Isaburo. Isaburo is a good man, but on the death of his wife, last year, he forsook his father-in-law and went back to his old home. It is principally for that reason that I am about to seek and remonstrate with him now.'

'Am I to understand,' said Kyuzaemon, 'that the daughter who was married to Isaburo was the one who perished in the snow last year? If so, you must be the spirit of Oyasu or Isaburo's wife?'

'Yes, that is right,' said the spirit. 'I was Oyasu, the wife of Isaburo, who perished now a year ago in the great snowstorm, of which tomorrow will be the anniversary.'

Kyuzaemon, with trembling hands, lit the lamp in the little *butsudan*, mumbling '*Namu Amida Butsu, Namu Amida Butsu*' with a fervour which he had never felt before. When this was done, he saw the figure of the *Yuki Onna* (Snow Ghost) advance, but there was no sound of footsteps as she glided to the altar.

Kyuzaemon retired to bed, where he promptly fell asleep; but shortly afterwards he was disturbed by the voice of the woman bidding him farewell. Before he had time to sit up she disappeared, leaving no sign; the fire still burned in the *butsudan*.

Kyuzaemon got up at daybreak and went to the next village to see Isaburo, whom he found living with his father-in-law, Yazaemon.

'Yes,' said Isaburo, 'it was wrong of me to leave my late wife's father when she died, and I am not surprised that on cold nights when it snows I have been visited continually by my wife's spirit as a reproof. Early this morning I saw her again, and I resolved to return. I have only been here two hours as it is.'

On comparing notes, Kyuzaemon and Isaburo found that directly the spirit of Oyasu had left the house of Kyuzaemon she appeared to Isaburo, at about half an hour after midnight, and stayed with him until he had promised to return to her father's house and help him to live in his old age.

That is roughly my story of the *Yuki Onna*. All those who die by the snow and cold become spirits of snow, appearing when there is snow; just as the spirits of those who are drowned in the sea only appear in stormy seas.

Even to the present day, in the north, priests say prayers to appease the spirits of those who have died by snow, and to prevent them from haunting people who are connected with them.

R. G. S.
1908

Jikininki

Once, when Musō Kokushi, a priest of the Zen sect, was journeying alone through the Province of Mino, he lost his way in a mountain district where there was nobody to direct him. For a long time he wandered about helplessly; and he was beginning to despair of finding shelter for the night, when he perceived, on the top of a hill lighted by the last rays of the sun, one of those little hermitages called *anjitsu*, which are built for solitary priests. It seemed to be in ruinous condition, but he hastened to it eagerly, and found that it was inhabited by an aged priest, from whom he begged the favour of a night's lodging. This the old man harshly refused; but he directed Musō to a certain hamlet, in the valley adjoining, where lodging and food could be obtained.

Musō found his way to the hamlet, which consisted of less than a dozen farm cottages, and he was kindly received at the dwelling of the headman. Forty or fifty persons were assembled in the principal apartment at the moment of Musō's arrival; but he was shown into a small, separate room, where he was promptly supplied with food and bedding. Being very tired, he lay down to rest at an early hour; but a little before midnight he was roused from sleep by a sound of loud weeping in the next apartment. Presently, the sliding screens were gently pushed apart and a young man, carrying a lighted lantern, entered the room, respectfully saluted him, and said:

'Reverend sir, it is my painful duty to tell you that I am now the responsible head of this house. Yesterday I was only the eldest son. But when you came here, tired as you were, we did not wish that you should feel embarrassed in any way: therefore, we did not tell you that Father had died only a few hours before. The people whom you saw in the next room are the inhabitants of this village: they all assembled here to pay their last respects to the dead; and now they are going to another village, about three miles off – for by our custom, no one of us may remain in this village during the night after a death has taken place. We make the proper offerings and prayers, then we go away, leaving the corpse alone. Strange things always happen in the house where a corpse has thus been left: so we think that it will be better for you to come away with us. We can find you good lodging in the other village. But perhaps, as you are a priest, you have no fear of demons or evil spirits; and, if you are not afraid of being left alone with the body, you will be very welcome to the use of this poor house. However, I must tell you that nobody, except a priest, would dare to remain here tonight.'

Musō made answer:

'For your kind intention and your generous hospitality, I am deeply grateful. But I am sorry that you did not tell me of your father's death when I came – for, though I was a little tired, I certainly was not so tired that I should have found difficulty in doing my duty as a priest. Had you told me, I could have performed the service before your departure. As it is, I shall perform the service after you have gone away, and I shall stay by the body until morning. I do not know what you mean by your words about the danger of staying here alone, but I am not afraid of ghosts or demons. Therefore, please to feel no anxiety on my account.'

The young man appeared to be rejoiced by these assurances, and expressed his gratitude in fitting words. Then the other members of the family, and the folk assembled in the adjoining room, having been told of the priest's kind promises, came to thank him – after which the master of the house said:

'Now, reverend sir, much as we regret to leave you alone, we must bid you farewell. By the rule of our village, none of us can stay here after midnight. We beg, kind sir, that you will take every care of your honourable body, while we are unable to attend upon you. And if you happen to hear or see anything strange during our absence, please tell us of the matter when we return in the morning.'

All then left the house, except the priest, who went to the room where the dead body was lying. The usual offerings had been set before the corpse, and a small Buddhist lamp (*tōmyō*) was burning. The priest recited the service and performed the funeral ceremonies – after which he entered into meditation. So meditating, he remained through several silent hours, and there was no sound in the deserted village. But when the hush of the night was at its deepest, there noiselessly entered a Shape, vague and vast; and in the same moment Musō found himself without power to move or speak. He saw that Shape lift the corpse, as with hands, devour it, more quickly than a cat devours a rat – beginning at the head and eating everything: the hair and the bones and even the shroud. And the monstrous Thing, having thus consumed the body, turned to the offerings and ate them also. Then it went away, as mysteriously as it had come.

When the villagers returned next morning, they found the priest awaiting them at the door of the headman's dwelling. All in turn saluted him; and, when they had entered and looked about the room, no one expressed any surprise at the disappearance of the dead body and the offerings. But the master of the house said to Musō:

'Reverend sir, you have probably seen unpleasant things during the night: all of us were anxious about you. But now we are very happy to find you alive and unharmed. Gladly we would have stayed with you, if it had been possible. But the law of our village, as I told you last evening, obliges us to quit our houses after a death has taken place, and to leave the corpse alone. Whenever this law has been broken, heretofore, some great misfortune has followed. Whenever it is obeyed, we find that the corpse and the offerings disappear during our absence. Perhaps you have seen the cause.'

Then Musō told of the dim and awful Shape that had entered the death chamber to devour the body and the offerings. No person seemed to be surprised by his narration; and the master of the house observed:

'What you have told us, reverend sir, agrees with what has been said about this matter from ancient time.'

Musō then inquired:

'Does not the priest on the hill sometimes perform the funeral service for your dead?'

'What priest?' the young man asked.

'The priest who yesterday evening directed me to this village,' answered Musō. 'I called at his *anjitsu* on the hill yonder. He refused me lodging, but told me the way here.'

The listeners looked at each other, as in astonishment; and, after a moment of silence, the master of the house said:

'Reverend sir, there is no priest and there is no *anjitsu* on the hill. For the time of many generations there has not been any resident priest in this neighbourhood.'

Musō said nothing more on the subject; for it was evident that his kind hosts supposed him to have been deluded by some goblin. But after having bidden them farewell, and obtained all necessary information as to his road, he determined to look again for the hermitage on the hill and so to ascertain whether he had really been deceived. He found the *anjitsu* without any difficulty; and, this time, its aged occupant invited him to enter. When he had done so, the hermit humbly bowed down before him, exclaiming: 'Ah! I am ashamed! – I am very much ashamed! – I am exceedingly ashamed!'

'You need not be ashamed for having refused me shelter,' said Musō. 'You directed me to the village yonder, where I was very kindly treated, and I thank you for that favour.'

'I can give no man shelter,' the recluse made answer, 'and it is not for the refusal that I am ashamed. I am ashamed only that you should have seen me in my real shape – for it was I who devoured the corpse and the offerings last night before your eyes ... Know, reverend sir, that I am a *jikininki* – an eater of human flesh. Have pity upon me, and suffer me to confess the secret fault by which I became reduced to this condition.

'A long, long time ago, I was a priest in this desolate region. There was no other priest for many leagues around. So, in that time, the bodies of the mountain folk who died used to be brought here – sometimes from great distances – in order that I might repeat over them the holy service. But I repeated the service and performed the rites only as a matter of business – I thought only of the food and the clothes that my sacred profession enabled me to gain. And because of this selfish impiety I was reborn, immediately after my death, into the state of a *jikininki*. Since then I have been obliged to feed upon the corpses of the people who die in this district: every one of them I must devour in the way that you saw last night ... Now, reverend sir, let me beseech you to perform a *Ségaki*-service for me: help me by your prayers, I entreat you, so that I may be soon able to escape from this horrible state of existence.'

No sooner had the hermit uttered this petition than he

disappeared; and the hermitage also disappeared at the same instant. And Musō Kokushi found himself kneeling alone in the high grass, beside an ancient and moss-grown tomb of the form called *go-rin-ishi*, which seemed to be the tomb of a priest.

L. H.

1904

A Haunted Temple in
Inaba Province

About the year 1680 there stood an old temple on a wild, pine-clad mountain near the village of Kisaichi, in the Province of Inaba. The temple was far up in a rocky ravine. So high and thick were the trees, they kept out nearly all daylight, even when the sun was at its highest. As long as the old men of the village could remember, the temple had been haunted by a *shito dama*★ and the skeleton ghost (they thought) of some former priestly occupant. Many priests had tried to live in the temple and make it their home, but all had died. No one could spend a night there and live.

At last, in the winter of 1701, there arrived at the village of Kisaichi a priest who was on a pilgrimage. His name was Jogen and he was a native of the Province of Kai.

Jogen had come to see the haunted temple. He was fond of studying such things. Though he believed in the *shito dama* form of spiritual return to earth, he did not believe in ghosts. As a matter of fact, he was anxious to see a *shito dama*, and, moreover, wished to have a temple of his own. In this wild mountain

★ The astral form a spirit can assume if it wishes to wander the earth after death.

temple, with a history which fear and death prevented people from visiting or priests inhabiting, he thought that he had (to put it in vulgar English) 'a real good thing'. Thus he had found his way to the village on the evening of a cold December night, and had gone to the inn to eat his rice and to hear all he could about the temple.

Jogen was no coward; on the contrary, he was a brave man and made all inquiries in the calmest manner.

'Sir,' said the landlord, 'your holiness must not think of going to this temple, for it means death. Many good priests have tried to stay the night there, and every one has been found next morning dead, or has died shortly after daybreak without coming to his senses. It is no use, sir, trying to defy such an evil spirit as comes to this temple. I beg you, sir, to give up the idea. Badly as we want a temple here, we wish for no more deaths, and often think of burning down this old haunted one and building a new.'

Jogen, however, was firm in his resolve to find and see the ghost.

'Kind sir,' he answered, 'your wishes are for my preservation; but it is my ambition to see a *shito dama*, and, if prayers can quiet it, to reopen the temple, to read its legends from the old books that must lie hidden therein, and to be the head priest of it, generally.'

The innkeeper, seeing that the priest was not to be dissuaded, gave up the attempt, and promised that his son should accompany him as guide in the morning and carry sufficient provisions for a day.

Next morning was one of brilliant sunshine, and Jogen was out of bed early, making preparations. Kosa, the innkeeper's twenty-year-old son, was tying up the priest's bedding and enough boiled rice to last him nearly two full days. It was decided that Kosa, after leaving the priest at the temple, should return to the village, for he as well as every other villager refused to spend a night at the weird place; but he and his father agreed to go and see Jogen on the morrow, or (as someone grimly put it) 'to carry him down and give him an honourable funeral and decent burial'.

Jogen entered fully into this joke, and shortly after left the village, with Kosa carrying his things and guiding the way.

The gorge in which the temple was situated was very steep and wild. Great moss-clad rocks lay strewn everywhere. When Jogen and his companion had got halfway up they sat down to rest and eat. Soon they heard voices of persons ascending, and ere long the innkeeper and some eight or nine of the village elders presented themselves.

'We have followed you,' said the innkeeper, 'to try once more to dissuade you from running to a sure death. True, we want the temple opened and the ghosts appeased, but we do not wish it at the cost of another life. Please consider!'

'I cannot change my mind,' answered the priest. 'Besides, this is the one chance of my life. Your village elders have promised me that if I am able to appease the spirit and reopen the temple I shall be the head priest of the temple, which must hereafter become celebrated.'

Again Jogen refused to listen to advice and laughed at the villagers' fears. Shouldering the packages that had been carried by Kosa, he said:

'Go back with the rest. I can find my own way now easily enough. I shall be glad if you return tomorrow with carpenters, for no doubt the temple is in sad want of repairs, both inside and out. Now, my friends, until tomorrow, farewell. Have no fear for me: I have none for myself.'

The villagers made deep bows. They were greatly impressed by the bravery of Jogen and hoped that he might be spared to become their priest. Jogen in his turn bowed and then began to continue his ascent. The others watched him as long as he

remained in view, and then retraced their steps to the village;
Kosa thanking the good fortune that had not necessitated his
having to go to the temple with the priest and return in the
evening alone. With two or three people he felt brave enough,
but to be here in the gloom of this wild forest and near the
haunted temple alone – no: that was not in his line.

As Jogen climbed he came suddenly in sight of the temple,
which seemed to be almost over his head, so precipitous were
the sides of the mountain and the path. Filled with curiosity, the
priest pressed on in spite of his heavy load, and some fifteen
minutes later arrived, panting, on the temple platform or ter-
race, which, like the temple itself, had been built on driven piles
and scaffolding.

At first glance Jogen recognised that the temple was large, but
lack of attention had caused it to fall into great dilapidation.
Rank grasses grew high about its sides; fungi and creepers
abounded upon the damp, sodden posts and supports; so rotten,
in fact, did these appear, the priest mentioned in his written
notes that evening that he feared the spirits less than the state of
the posts which supported the building.

Cautiously, Jogen entered the temple and saw that there was
a remarkably large and fine gilded figure of Buddha, besides figures of many saints. There were also fine bronzes and vases,
drums from which the parchment had rotted off, incense-
burners or *koros*, and other valuable or holy things.

Behind the temple were the priests' living quarters; evidently, before the ghost's time, the temple must have had some
five or six priests ever present to attend to it and to the people
who came to pray.

The gloom was oppressive, and, as the evening was already
approaching, Jogen bethought himself of light. Unpacking his
bundle, he filled a lamp with oil and found temple-sticks for the
candles which he had brought with him. Having placed one of

these on either side of the figure of Buddha, he prayed earnestly for two hours, by which time it was quite dark. Then he took his simple meal of rice and settled himself to watch and listen. In order that he might see inside and outside the temple at the same time, he had chosen the gallery. Concealed behind an old column, he waited, in his heart disbelieving in ghosts, but anxious, as his notes said, to see a *shito dama*.

For some two hours he heard nothing. The wind – such little as there was – sighed around the temple and through the stems of the tall trees. An owl hooted from time to time. Bats flew in and out. A fungusy smell pervaded the air.

Suddenly, near midnight, Jogen heard a rustling in the bushes below him, as if somebody were pushing through. He thought it was a deer, or perhaps one of the large, red-faced apes so fond of the neighbourhood of high and deserted temples; perhaps, even, it might be a fox or a badger.

The priest was soon undeceived. At the place whence the sound of the rustling leaves had come, he saw the clear and distinct shape of the well-known *shito dama*. It moved first one way and then another, in a hovering and jerky manner, and from it a voice as of distant buzzing proceeded; but – horror of horrors! – what was that standing among the bushes?

The priest's blood ran cold. There stood the luminous skeleton of a man in loose priest's clothes, with glaring eyes and a parchment skin! At first it remained still, but as the *shito dama* rose higher and higher, the ghost moved after it – sometimes visible, sometimes not.

Higher and higher came the *shito dama*, until finally the ghost stood at the base of the great figure of Buddha, and was facing Jogen.

Cold beads of sweat stood out on the priest's forehead; the marrow seemed to have frozen in his bones; he shook so that he could hardly stand. Biting his tongue to prevent screaming, he dashed for the small room in which he had left his bedding, and, having bolted himself in, proceeded to look through a crack between the boards. Yes! There was the figure of the ghost, still seated near the Buddha; but the *shito dama* had disappeared.

None of Jogen's senses left him, but fear was paralysing his body, and he felt himself no longer capable of moving – no matter what should happen. He continued, in a lying position, to look through the hole.

The ghost sat on, turning only its head, sometimes to the right, sometimes to the left, and sometimes looking upwards.

For fully an hour this went on. Then the buzzing sound began again, and the *shito dama* reappeared, circling and circling around the ghost's body, until the ghost vanished, apparently having turned into the *shito dama*; and after circling around the holy figures three or four times it suddenly shot out of sight.

Next morning Kosa and five men came up to the temple. They found the priest alive but paralysed. He could neither move nor speak. He was carried to the village, dying before he got there.

Much use was made of the priest's notes. No one else ever volunteered to live at the temple, which, two years later, was struck by lightning and burned to the ground. In digging among the remains, searching for bronzes and metal Buddhas, villagers came upon a skeleton buried, only a foot deep, near the bushes whence Jogen had first heard the sounds of rustling.

Undoubtedly, the ghost and *shito dama* were those of a priest who had suffered a violent death and could not rest.

The bones were properly buried and masses said, and nothing has since been seen of the ghost.

All that remains of the temple are the moss-grown pedestals which formed the foundations.

R. G. S.
1908

The Camphor Tree Tomb

Five *ri* (ten miles) from Shirakawa, in the Province of Iwaki, there is a village called Yabuki-mura. Close by is a grove some 400 feet square. The trees used to include a monster camphor nearly 150 feet in height, of untold age, and venerated by villagers and strangers alike as one of the greatest trees in Japan. A shrine was erected to it in the grove, which was known as the Nekoma-Myojin Forest; and a faithful old man, Hamada Tsushima, lived there, caring for the tree, the shrine and the whole grove.

One day the tree was felled; but, instead of withering or dying, it continued to grow, and it is still flourishing, though lying on the ground. Poor Hamada Tsushima disembowelled himself when the sacred tree had been cut down. Perhaps it is because his spirit entered the sacred tree that the tree will not die. Here is the story:

On the 17th of January in the third and last year of the Meireki period – that is, 1658 – a great fire broke out in the Homyoji Temple in the Maruyama Hongō district of Tokyo. The fire spread with such rapidity that not only was that particular district burned, but also a full eighth of Tokyo itself was destroyed. Many of the daimios' houses and palaces were consumed. The Lord Date Tsunamune of Sendai, one of the three greatest daimios (who were Satsuma, Kaga, Sendai), had the whole of his seven palaces and houses destroyed by the fire; the other daimios or feudal lords lost only one or two.

Lord Date Tsunamune resolved to build the finest palace that could be designed. It was to be at Shinzenza, in Shiba. He ordered that no time should be lost, and directed one of his high officials, Harada Kai Naonori, to see to the matter. Harada, accordingly, sent for the greatest house-building contractor of the day, one Kinokuniya Bunzaemon, and to him he said:

'You are aware that the fire has destroyed the whole of the town mansions of Lord Date Tsunamune. I am directed to see that the finest palace should be built immediately, second to none except the Shogun's. I have sent for you as the largest contractor in Tokyo. What can you do? Just make some suggestions and give me your opinion.'

'Certainly, my lord, I can make plenty of suggestions; but to build such a palace will cost an enormous amount of money, especially now, after this fire, for there is a great scarcity of large timber in the land.'

'Never mind expenses,' said Harada. 'Those I shall pay as you like and when you like. I will even advance money if you want it.'

'Oh, then,' answered the delighted contractor, 'I will start immediately. What would you think of having a palace like that of Kinkakuji in Kyoto, which was built by the Shogun Ashikaga? What I should build would be a finer mansion than that of the present Shogun — let alone those of any daimio. The whole of the *hagi* (shelves) to be made out of the rarest woods; the *tokobashira* (corner post) to be of the *nanten*, and ceilings of unjointed camphor-tree boards, should we be able to find a tree of sufficient size. I can find nearly everything, except the last, in my own stocks; the camphor trees are difficult. There are but few; they are mostly sacred and dangerous to interfere with or obtain. I know of one in the forest of Nekoma-Myojin in Iwaki

Province. If I can get that tree, I should indeed be able to make an unjointed ceiling, and that would completely put other palaces and mansions in the second rank.'

'Well, well, I must leave all this to you,' said Harada. 'You know that no expense need be spared, so long as you produce speedily what is required by Lord Date Tsunamune.'

The contractor bowed low, saying that he should set to and do his best; and he left, no doubt, delighted at so open a contract, which would enable him to fill his pockets. He set about making inquiries in every direction, and became convinced that the only camphor tree that would suit his purpose was the one before referred to – owing chiefly to its great breadth. Kinokuniya knew also that the part of the district wherein lay this tree belonged to or was under the management of Fujieda Geki, now in the Hongō district of Tokyo acting as a Shogun's retainer; well off (receiving 1,200 *koku* of rice a year), but not over scrupulous about money, of which he was always in need.

Contractor Kinokuniya soon learned all about the man, and then went to call.

'Your name is Kinokuniya Bunzaemon, I believe. What, may I ask, do you wish to see me about?' said Fujieda.

'Sir,' said the contractor, bowing low, 'it is as you say. My name is Kinokuniya Bunzaemon and I am a wood contractor of whom perhaps your lordship has heard, for I have built and supplied the wood for many mansions and palaces. I come here craving assistance in the way of permission to cut trees in a small forest called Nekoma-Myojin, near the village called Yabukimura in the Sendai district.'

The contractor did not tell Fujieda Geki, the Shogun's retainer or agent, that he was to build a mansion for the daimio Date Tsunamune, and that the wood which he wanted to cut was within that daimio's domains. For he knew full well that the Lord Date would never give him permission to cut a holy tree.

It was an excellent idea to take the daimio's trees by the help of the Shogun's agent, and charge for them fully afterwards. So he continued:

'I can assure you, sir, this recent fire has cleared the whole market of wood. If you will assist me to get what I want, I will build you a new house for nothing, and by way of showing my appreciation, I ask you to accept this small gift of yen 200, which is only a little beginning.'

'You need not trouble with these small details,' said the delighted agent, pocketing the money, 'but do as you wish. I will send for the four local managers and headmen of the district wherein you wish to cut the trees, and I will let you know when they arrive in Tokyo. With them you will be able to settle the matter.'

The interview was over. The contractor was on the high road, he felt, to getting the trees he required, and the money-wanting agent was equally well pleased that so slight an effort on his part should have been the means of enriching him by yen 200, with the promise of more and a new house.

About ten days later four men, the heads of villages, arrived in Tokyo and presented themselves to Fujieda, who sent for the timber contractor, telling the four – whose names were Mosuke, Magozaemon, Yohei and Jinyemon – that he was pleased to see them and to note how loyal they had been in their attendance on the Shogun, for that he – the Shogun – had had his palace burned down in the recent fire, and desired to have one immediately built, the great and only difficulty being the timber.

'I am told by our great contractor, to whom I shall introduce you presently, that the only timber fit for rebuilding the Shogun's palace lies in your district. I myself know nothing about these details, and I shall leave you gentlemen to settle these matters with Kinokuniya, the contractor, so soon as he arrives. I have sent for him. In the meantime, consider yourselves welcome, and please accept of the meal I have arranged in the next room for you. Come along and let us enjoy it.'

Fujieda led the four countrymen into the next room, and ate with them at the meal, during which time Kinokuniya the contractor arrived, and was promptly ushered into their presence. The meal was nearly at an end.

Fujieda introduced the contractor, who in his turn said:

'Gentlemen, we cannot discuss these matters here in the house of Lord Fujieda, the Shogun's agent. Now that we know one another, let me invite you to supper; at that I can explain to you exactly what I want in the way of trees out of your district. Of course, you know my family are subjects of your feudal lords, and that we are therefore all the same.'

The four countrymen were delighted at so much hospitality. Two meals in an evening was an extraordinary dissipation for them, and that in Tokyo! My word, what would they not be able to tell their wives on their return to the villages?

Kinokuniya led the four countrymen off to a restaurant called Kampanaro in Ryogoku, where he treated them with the greatest hospitality. After the meal he said:

'Gentlemen, I hope you will allow me to hew timber from the forest in your village, for it is impossible for me otherwise to attempt any further building on a large scale.'

'Very well, you may hew,' said Mosuke, who was the senior of the four. 'Since the cutting of the trees in Nekoma-Myojin Forest is as it were a necessity for our lord, they must be cut; it is, in fact, I take it, an order from our lord that the trees shall be cut; but I must remind you that there is one tree in the grove which cannot be cut amid any circumstances whatever, and that is an enormous and sacred camphor tree which is very much revered in our district, and to which a shrine is erected. That tree we cannot consent to have cut.'

'Very well,' said the contractor. 'Just write me a little permit, giving me permission to cut any trees except the big camphor, and our business will be finished.'

Kinokuniya had by this time in the evening taken his measure of the countrymen – so shrewdly as to know that they were probably unable to write.

'Certainly,' said Mosuke. 'Just you write out a little agreement, Jinyemon.'

'No, I would rather you wrote it, Mago,' said Jinyemon.

'And I should like Yohei to write it,' said Mago.

'But I can't write at all,' said Yohei, turning to Jinyemon again.

'Well, never mind, never mind,' said Kinokuniya. 'Will you gentlemen sign the document if I write it?'

Why, of course, they all assented. That was the best way of all. They would put their stamps to the document. This they did, and, after a lively evening, departed pleased with themselves generally.

Kinokuniya, on the other hand, went home fully contented with his evening's business. Had he not in his pocket the permit to cut the trees, and had he not written it himself, so as to suit his own purpose? He chuckled at the thought of how neatly he had managed the business.

Next morning Kinokuniya sent off his foreman Chogoro, accompanied by ten or a dozen men. It took them three days to reach the village called Yabuki-mura, near the Nekoma-Myojin Forest. They arrived on the morning of the fourth day, and proceeded to erect a scaffold around the camphor tree, so that they might the better use their axes. As they began chopping off the lower branches, Hamada Tsushima, the keeper of the shrine, came running to them.

'Here, here! What are you doing? Cutting down the sacred camphor? Curse you! Stop, I tell you! Do you hear me? Stop at once!'

Chogoro answered:

'You need not stop my men in their work. They are doing what they have been ordered to do, and with a full right to do it. I am cutting down the tree at the order of my master Kinokuniya, the timber contractor, who has permission to cut the tree from the four headmen sent to Tokyo from this district.'

'I know all that,' said the caretaker, 'but your permission is to cut down any tree except the sacred camphor.'

'There you are wrong, as this letter will show you,' said Chogoro. 'Read it yourself.' And the caretaker, in great dismay, read as follows:

> To Kinokuniya Bunzaemon,
> Timber Contractor, Tokyo.
>
> In hewing trees to build a new mansion for our lord, all the camphor trees must be spared, except the large one said to be sacred in the Nekoma-Myojin Forest. In witness whereof we set our names.
>
> JINYEMON   MAGOZAEMON   MOSUKE   YOHEI
> Representing the local County Officials.

The caretaker, beside himself with grief and astonishment, sent for the four men mentioned. On their arrival, each declared that he had given permission to cut anything except the big camphor; but Chogoro said that he could not believe them, and in any case he would go by the written document. Then he ordered his men to continue their work on the big camphor.

Hamada Tsushima, the caretaker, did hara-kiri, disembowelling himself there and then; but not before telling Chogoro that his spirit would go into the camphor tree, to take care of it, and to wreak vengeance on the wicked Kinokuniya.

At last the efforts of the men brought the stately tree down with a crash; but then they found themselves unable to move it.

Pull as they might, it would not budge. Each time they tried, the branches seemed to become alive; faces and eyes became painful with the hits they got from them. Pluckily, they continued their efforts, but it was no use. Things got worse. Several of the men were caught and nearly crushed to death between the branches; four had broken limbs from blows given in the same way. At this moment a horseman rode up and shouted:

'My name is Matsumaye Tetsunosuke. I am one of the Lord of Sendai's retainers. The board of councillors in Sendai have refused to allow this camphor tree to be touched. You have cut it, unfortunately. It must now remain where it is. Our feudal lord of Sendai, Lord Date Tsunamune, will be furious. Kinokuniya the contractor planned an evil scheme and will be duly punished; while as for the Shogun's agent, Fujieda Geki, he also must be reported. You yourselves return to Tokyo. We cannot blame you for obeying orders. But first give me that forged permit signed by the four local fools, who, it is trusted, will destroy themselves.'

Chogoro and his men returned to Tokyo. A few days later the contractor was taken ill and a shampooer was sent to his room. A little later Kinokuniya was found dead; the shampooer had disappeared, though it was impossible for him to have got away without being seen! It is said that the spirit of Hamada Tsushima, the caretaker, had taken the form of the shampooer in order to kill the contractor. Chogoro became so uneasy in his mind that he returned to the camphor tree, where he spent all his savings in erecting a new shrine and putting in a caretaker. This is known as the *Kusunoki Dzuka* (Camphor Tree Tomb). The tree lies there, my storyteller tells me, at the present day.

R. G. S.
1908

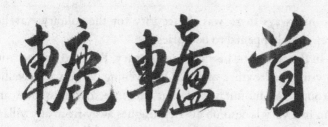

Rokurokubi

Nearly 500 years ago there was a samurai named Isogai Héï-
dazaëmon Takétsura, in the service of the Lord Kikuji, of
Kyūshū. This Isogai had inherited, from many warlike ancestors, a natural aptitude for military exercises and extraordinary
strength. While yet a boy he had surpassed his teachers in the art
of swordsmanship, in archery, and in the use of the spear, and
had displayed all the capacities of a daring and skilful soldier.
Afterwards, in the time of the Eikyō War, he so distinguished
himself that high honours were bestowed upon him. But when
the house of Kikuji came to ruin, Isogai found himself without
a master. He might then easily have obtained service under
another daimio; but as he had never sought distinction for his
own sake alone, and as his heart remained true to his former
lord, he preferred to give up the world. So he cut off his hair and
became a travelling priest – taking the Buddhist name of
Kwairyō.

But always, under the *koromo* (robe) of the priest, Kwairyō
kept warm within him the heart of the samurai. As in other
years he had laughed at peril, so now also he scorned danger;
and in all weathers and all seasons he journeyed to preach the
good Law in places where no other priest would have dared to
go. For that age was an age of violence and disorder; and upon

the highways there was no security for the solitary traveller, even if he happened to be a priest.

In the course of his first long journey, Kwairyō had occasion to visit the Province of Kai. One evening, as he was travelling through the mountains of that province, darkness overcame him in a very lonesome district, leagues away from any village. So he resigned himself to pass the night under the stars; and, having found a suitable grassy spot by the roadside, he lay down there and prepared to sleep. He had always welcomed discomfort; and even a bare rock was for him a good bed, when nothing better could be found, and the root of a pine tree an excellent pillow. His body was iron and he never troubled himself about dews or rain or frost or snow.

Scarcely had he lain down when a man came along the road, carrying an axe and a great bundle of chopped wood. This woodcutter halted on seeing Kwairyō lying down, and, after a moment of silent observation, said to him in a tone of great surprise:

'What kind of a man can you be, good sir, that you dare to lie down alone in such a place as this? . . . There are haunters about here – many of them. Are you not afraid of Hairy Things?'

'My friend,' cheerfully answered Kwairyō, 'I am only a wandering priest – a "Cloud-and-Water-Guest", as folks call it: *Unsui-no-ryokaku*. And I am not in the least afraid of Hairy Things – if you mean goblin-foxes or goblin-badgers or any creatures of that kind. As for lonesome places, I like them: they are suitable for meditation. I am accustomed to sleeping in the open air and I have learned never to be anxious about my life.'

'You must be indeed a brave man, Sir Priest,' the peasant responded, 'to lie down here! This place has a bad name – a very bad name. But as the proverb has it, *Kunshi ayayuki ni chikayorazu* (The superior man does not needlessly expose himself to peril); and I must assure you, sir, that it is very dangerous to sleep here.

Therefore, although my house is only a wretched thatched hut, let me beg of you to come home with me at once. In the way of food, I have nothing to offer you; but there is a roof at least, and you can sleep under it without risk.'

He spoke earnestly, and Kwairyō, liking the kindly tone of the man, accepted this modest offer. The woodcutter guided him along a narrow path, leading up from the main road through mountain forest. It was a rough and dangerous path – sometimes skirting precipices; sometimes offering nothing but a network of slippery roots for the foot to rest upon; sometimes winding over or between masses of jagged rock. But at last Kwairyō found himself upon a cleared space at the top of a hill with a full moon shining overhead; and he saw before him a small thatched cottage, cheerfully lighted from within. The woodcutter led him to a shed at the back of the house, whither water had been conducted, through bamboo pipes, from some neighbouring stream; and the two men washed their feet. Beyond the shed was a vegetable garden, and a grove of cedars and bamboos; and beyond the trees appeared the glimmer of a cascade, pouring from some loftier height and swaying in the moonshine like a long white robe.

As Kwairyō entered the cottage with his guide, he perceived four persons – men and women – warming their hands at a little fire kindled in the *ro* (fireplace) of the principal apartment. They bowed low to the priest and greeted him in the most respectful manner. Kwairyō wondered that persons so poor, and dwelling in such a solitude, should be aware of the polite forms of greeting. 'These are good people,' he thought to himself, 'and they must have been taught by someone well acquainted with the rules of propriety.' Then, turning to his host – the *aruji* or house-master, as the others called him – Kwairyō said:

'From the kindness of your speech, and from the very polite welcome given me by your household, I imagine that you have not always been a woodcutter. Perhaps you formerly belonged to one of the upper classes?'

Smiling, the woodcutter answered:

'Sir, you are not mistaken. Though now living as you find me, I was once a person of some distinction. My story is the story of a ruined life – ruined by my own fault. I used to be in the service of a daimio, and my rank in that service was not inconsiderable. But I loved women and wine too well; and under the influence of passion I acted wickedly. My selfishness brought about the ruin of our house and caused the death of many persons. Retribution followed me and I long remained a fugitive in the land. Now I often pray that I may be able to make some atonement for the evil which I did, and to re-establish the ancestral home. But I fear that I shall never find any way of so doing. Nevertheless, I try to overcome the karma of my errors by sincere repentance, and by helping, as far as I can, those who are unfortunate.'

Kwairyō was pleased by this announcement of good resolve, and he said to the *aruji*:

'My friend, I have had occasion to observe that men, prone to folly in their youth, may in after years become very earnest in right-living. In the holy sutras it is written that those strongest in wrongdoing can become, by power of good resolve, the strongest in right-doing. I do not doubt that you have a good heart; and I hope that better fortune will come to you. Tonight I shall recite the sutras for your sake, and pray that you may obtain the force to overcome the karma of any past errors.'

With these assurances, Kwairyō bade the *aruji* goodnight; and his host showed him to a very small side room, where a bed had been made ready. Then all went to sleep, except the priest, who began to read the sutras by the light of a paper lantern. Until a late hour he continued to read and pray: then he opened a little window in his little sleeping-room, to take a last look at the landscape before lying down. The night was beautiful: there was no cloud in the sky; there was no wind; and the strong moonlight threw down sharp black shadows of foliage and glittered on the dews of the garden. Shrillings of crickets and bell-insects made a musical tumult; and the sound of the neighbouring cascade deepened with the night. Kwairyō felt thirsty as he listened to the noise of the water; and, remembering the bamboo aqueduct at the rear of the house, he thought that he could go there and get a drink without disturbing the sleeping household. Very gently, he pushed apart the sliding screens that separated his room from the main apartment; and he saw, by the light of the lantern, five recumbent bodies – without heads!

For one instant he stood bewildered, imagining a crime. But in another moment he perceived that there was no blood, and that the headless necks did not look as if they had been cut. Then he thought to himself: 'Either this is an illusion made by goblins or I have been lured into the dwelling of a *Rokurokubi* . . . In the book *Sōshinki* it is written that if one finds the body of a *Rokurokubi* without its head, and removes the body to another place, the head will never be able to join itself again to the neck. And the book further says that when the head comes back and finds that its body has been moved, it will strike itself upon the floor three times – bounding like a ball – and will pant as in great fear and presently die. Now, if these be *Rokurokubi*, they mean me no good – so I shall be justified in following the instructions of the book.'

He seized the body of the *aruji* by the feet, pulled it to the window and pushed it out. Then he went to the back door, which he found barred; and he surmised that the heads had made their exit through the smoke-hole in the roof, which had been left open. Gently unbarring the door, he made his way to the garden and proceeded with all possible caution to the grove beyond it. He heard voices talking in the grove, and he went in the direction of the voices – stealing from shadow to shadow, until he reached a good hiding place. Then, from behind a trunk, he caught sight of the heads – all five of them – flitting about and chatting as they flitted. They were eating worms and insects, which they found on the ground or among the trees. Presently, the head of the *aruji* stopped eating and said:

'Ah, that travelling priest who came tonight! – how fat all his body is! When we shall have eaten him, our bellies will be well filled . . . I was foolish to talk to him as I did – it only set him to reciting the sutras on behalf of my soul! To go near him while he is reciting would be difficult, and we cannot touch him so long as he is praying. But as it is now nearly morning, perhaps he has gone to sleep . . . Some one of you go to the house and see what the fellow is doing.'

Another head – the head of a young woman – immediately rose up and flitted to the house, as lightly as a bat. After a few minutes it came back and cried out huskily in a tone of great alarm:

'That travelling priest is not in the house – he is gone! But that is not the worst of the matter. He has taken the body of our *aruji* and I do not know where he has put it.'

At this announcement the head of the *aruji* – distinctly visible in the moonlight – assumed a frightful aspect: its eyes opened monstrously, its hair stood up bristling and its teeth gnashed. Then a cry burst from its lips, and – weeping tears of rage – it exclaimed:

'Since my body has been moved, to rejoin it is not possible! Then I must die! . . . And all through the work of that priest! Before I die I will get at that priest! – I will tear him! – I will devour him! . . . *And there he is* – behind that tree! – hiding behind that tree! See him! – the fat coward!'

In the same moment the head of the *aruji*, followed by the other four heads, sprang at Kwairyō. But the strong priest had already armed himself by plucking up a young tree; and with that tree he struck the heads as they came, knocking them from him with tremendous blows. Four of them fled away. But the head of the *aruji*, though battered again and again, desperately continued to bound at the priest, and at last caught him by the left sleeve of his robe. Kwairyō, however, as quickly gripped the head by its topknot and repeatedly struck it. It did not release its hold, but it uttered a long moan and thereafter ceased to struggle. It was dead. But its teeth still held the sleeve, and, for all his great strength, Kwairyō could not force open the jaws.

With the head still hanging to his sleeve he went back to the house, and there caught sight of the other four *Rokurokubi* squatting together, with their bruised and bleeding heads reunited to their bodies. But when they perceived him at the back door, all screamed, 'The priest! The priest!' – and fled through the other doorway, out into the woods.

Eastward, the sky was brightening; day was about to dawn; and Kwairyō knew that the power of the goblins was limited to the hours of darkness. He looked at the head clinging to his sleeve, its face all fouled with blood and foam and clay; and he laughed aloud as he thought to himself: 'What a *miyagé* (present)! – the head of a goblin!' After which, he gathered together his few belongings and leisurely descended the mountain to continue his journey.

Right on he journeyed, until he came to Suwa in Shinano; and into the main street of Suwa he solemnly strode, with the head dangling at his elbow. Then woman fainted, and children screamed and ran away; and there was a great crowding and clamouring until the *torité* (as the police in those days were called) seized the priest and took him to jail. For they supposed the head to be the head of a murdered man, who, in the moment of being killed, had caught the murderer's sleeve in his teeth. As for Kwairyō, he only smiled and said nothing when they questioned him. So, after having passed a night in prison, he was brought before the magistrates of the district. Then he was ordered to explain how he, a priest, had been found with the head of a man fastened to his sleeve, and why he had dared thus shamelessly to parade his crime in the sight of people.

Kwairyō laughed long and loudly at these questions; and then he said:

'Sirs, I did not fasten the head to my sleeve: it fastened itself there – much against my will. And I have not committed any crime. For this is not the head of a man; it is the head of a goblin – and, if I caused the death of the goblin, I did not do so by any shedding of blood, but simply by taking the precautions necessary to assure my own safety.' And he proceeded to relate the whole of the adventure, bursting into another hearty laugh as he told of his encounter with the five heads.

But the magistrates did not laugh. They judged him to be a hardened criminal, and his story an insult to their intelligence. Therefore, without further questioning, they decided to order his immediate execution – all of them except one, a very old man. This aged officer had made no remark during the trial; but, after having heard the opinion of his colleagues, he rose up and said:

'Let us first examine the head carefully; for this, I think, has not yet been done. If the priest has spoken truth, the head itself should bear witness for him . . . Bring the head here!'

So the head, still holding in its teeth the *koromo* that had been stripped from Kwairyō's shoulders, was put before the judges. The old man turned it around and around, carefully examined it, and discovered, on the nape of its neck, several strange red characters. He called the attention of his colleagues to these, and also bade them observe that the edges of the neck nowhere presented the appearance of having been cut by any weapon. On the contrary, the line of severance was smooth as the line at which a falling leaf detaches itself from the stem . . . Then said the elder:

'I am quite sure that the priest told us nothing but the truth. This is the head of a *Rokurokubi*. In the book *Nan-hō-ï-butsu-shi* it is written that certain red characters can always be found upon the nape of the neck of a real *Rokurokubi*. There are the characters: you can see for yourselves that they have not been painted. Moreover, it is well known that such goblins have been dwelling in the mountains of the Province of Kai from very ancient time . . . But you, sir,' he exclaimed, turning to Kwairyō, 'what sort of sturdy priest may you be? Certainly, you have given proof of a courage that few priests possess; and you have the air of a soldier rather than a priest. Perhaps you once belonged to the samurai class?'

'You have guessed rightly, sir,' Kwairyō responded. 'Before becoming a priest, I long followed the profession of arms; and in those days I never feared man or devil. My name then was Isogai Hêïdazaëmon Takétsura of Kyūshū. There may be some among you who remember it.'

At the mention of that name, a murmur of admiration filled the courtroom, for there were many present who remembered it. And Kwairyō immediately found himself among friends instead of judges – friends anxious to prove their admiration by fraternal kindness. With honour they escorted him to the residence of the daimio, who welcomed him and feasted him, and made him a handsome present before allowing him to depart. When Kwairyō left Suwa, he was as happy as any priest is permitted to be in this transitory world. As for the head, he took it with him, jocosely insisting that he intended it for a *miyagé*.

And now it only remains to tell what became of the head.

A day or two after leaving Suwa, Kwairyō met with a robber, who stopped him in a lonesome place and bade him strip. Kwairyō at once removed his *koromo* and offered it to the robber, who then first perceived what was hanging to the sleeve. Though brave, the highwayman was startled. He dropped the garment and sprang back. Then he cried out:

'You! – what kind of a priest are you? Why, you are a worse man than I am! It is true that I have killed people; but I never walked about with anybody's head fastened to my sleeve . . . Well, Sir Priest, I suppose we are of the same calling, and I must say that I admire you! . . . Now that head would be of use to me: I could frighten people with it. Will you sell it? You can have my robe in exchange for your *koromo*, and I will give you five *ryō* for the head.'

Kwairyō answered:

'I shall let you have the head and the robe if you insist, but I must tell you that this is not the head of a man. It is a goblin's head. So, if you buy it and have any trouble in consequence, please to remember that you were not deceived by me.'

'What a nice priest you are!' exclaimed the robber. 'You kill men and jest about it! . . . But I am really in earnest. Here is my robe and here is the money – and let me have the head . . . What is the use of joking?'

'Take the thing,' said Kwairyō. 'I was not joking. The only joke – if there be any joke at all – is that you are fool enough to pay good money for a goblin's head.' And Kwairyō, loudly laughing, went upon his way.

Thus the robber got the head and the *koromo*; and for some time he played goblin-priest upon the highways. But, reaching the neighbourhood of Suwa, he there learned the true story of the head; and he then became afraid that the spirit of the *Rokurokubi* might give him trouble. So he made up his mind to take back the head to the place from which it had come, and to bury it with its body. He found his way to the lonely cottage in the mountains of Kai; but nobody was there and he could not discover the body. Therefore, he buried the head by itself in the grove behind the cottage; and he had a tombstone set up over the grave; and he caused a *Ségaki*-service to be performed on behalf of the spirit of the *Rokurokubi*. And that tombstone – known as the Tombstone of the *Rokurokubi* – may be seen (at least, so the Japanese storyteller declares) even unto this day.

L. H.
1904

How an Old Man Lost His Wen

Many, many years ago there lived a good old man who had a wen like a tennis ball growing out of his right cheek. This lump was a great disfigurement to the old man, and so annoyed him that for many years he spent all his time and money in trying to get rid of it. He tried everything he could think of. He consulted many doctors, far and near, and took all kinds of medicines both internally and externally. But it was all of no use. The lump only grew bigger and bigger till it was nearly as big as his face, and in despair he gave up all hopes of ever losing it, and resigned himself to the thought of having to carry the lump on his face all his life.

One day the firewood gave out in his kitchen, so, as his wife wanted some at once, the old man took his axe and set out for the woods up among the hills not very far from his home. It was a fine day in the early autumn, and the old man enjoyed the fresh air and was in no hurry to get home. So the whole afternoon passed quickly while he was chopping wood, and he had collected a goodly pile to take back to his wife. When the day began to draw to a close, he turned his face homewards.

The old man had not gone far on his way down the mountain pass when the sky clouded and rain began to fall heavily. He looked about for some shelter, but there was not even a charcoal-burner's hut near. At last he espied a large hole in the hollow trunk of a tree. The hole was near the ground, so he crept in easily, and sat down in hopes that he had only been overtaken by a mountain shower and that the weather would soon clear.

But much to the old man's disappointment, instead of clearing, the rain fell more and more heavily, and finally a heavy thunderstorm broke over the mountain. The thunder roared so terrifically, and the heavens seemed to be so ablaze with lightning, that the old man could hardly believe himself to be alive. He thought that he must die of fright. At last, however, the sky cleared and the whole country was aglow in the rays of the setting sun. The old man's spirits revived when he looked out at the beautiful twilight, and he was about to step out from his strange hiding place in the hollow tree when the sound of what seemed like the approaching steps of several people caught his ear. He at once thought that his friends had come to look for him, and he was delighted at the idea of having some jolly companions with whom to walk home. But on looking out from the tree, what was his amazement to see, not his friends, but hundreds of demons coming towards the spot. The more he looked, the greater was his astonishment. Some of these demons were as large as giants, others had great big eyes out of all proportion to the rest of their bodies, others again had absurdly long noses, and some had such big mouths that they seemed to open from ear to ear. All had horns growing on their foreheads. The old man was so surprised at what he saw that he lost his balance and fell out of the hollow tree. Fortunately for him, the demons did not see him, as the tree was in the background. So he picked himself up and crept back into the tree.

While he was sitting there and wondering impatiently when he would be able to get home, he heard the sounds of gay music, and then some of the demons began to sing.

'What are these creatures doing?' said the old man to himself. 'I will look out, it sounds very amusing.'

On peeping out, the old man saw that the demon chief himself was actually sitting with his back against the tree in which he had taken refuge, and all the other demons were sitting around, some drinking and some dancing. Food and wine was spread before them on the ground, and the demons were evidently having a great entertainment and enjoying themselves immensely.

It made the old man laugh to see their strange antics.

'How amusing this is!' laughed the old man to himself. 'I am now quite old, but I have never seen anything so strange in all my life.'

He was so interested and excited in watching all that the demons were doing, that he forgot himself and stepped out of the tree and stood looking on.

The demon chief was just taking a big cup of sake and watching one of the demons dancing. In a little while, he said with a bored air:

'Your dance is rather monotonous. I am tired of watching it. Isn't there any one amongst you all who can dance better than this fellow?'

Now the old man had been fond of dancing all his life, and was quite an expert in the art, and he knew that he could do much better than the demon.

'Shall I go and dance before these demons and let them see what a human being can do? It may be dangerous, for if I don't please them they may kill me!' said the old fellow to himself.

His fears, however, were soon overcome by his love of dancing. In a few minutes he could restrain himself no longer, and came out before the whole party of demons and began to dance at once. The old man, realising that his life probably depended on whether he pleased these strange creatures or not, exerted his skill and wit to the utmost.

The demons were at first very surprised to see a man so fearlessly taking part in their entertainment, and then their surprise soon gave place to admiration.

'How strange!' exclaimed the horned chief. 'I never saw such a skilful dancer before! He dances admirably!'

When the old man had finished his dance, the big demon said:

'Thank you very much for your amusing dance. Now give us the pleasure of drinking a cup of wine with us,' and with these words he handed him his largest wine cup.

The old man thanked him very humbly:

'I did not expect such kindness from your lordship. I fear I have only disturbed your pleasant party by my unskilful dancing.'

'No, no,' answered the big demon. 'You must come often and dance for us. Your skill has given us much pleasure.'

The old man thanked him again and promised to do so.

'Then will you come again tomorrow, old man?' asked the demon.

'Certainly, I will,' answered the old man.

'Then you must leave some pledge of your word with us,' said the demon.

'Whatever you like,' said the old man.

'Now what is the best thing he can leave with us as a pledge?' asked the demon, looking around.

Then said one of the demon's attendants, kneeling behind the chief:

'The token he leaves with us must be the most important thing to him in his possession. I see the old man has a wen on his right cheek. Now mortal men consider such a wen very fortunate. Let my lord take the lump from the old man's right cheek, and he will surely come tomorrow, if only to get that back.'

'You are very clever,' said the demon chief, giving his horns an approving nod. Then he stretched out a hairy arm and claw-like hand, and took the great lump from the old man's right cheek. Strange to say, it came off as easily as a ripe plum from the tree at the demon's touch, and then the merry troop of demons suddenly vanished.

The old man was lost in bewilderment by all that had happened. He hardly knew for some time where he was. When he came to understand what had happened to him, he was delighted to find that the lump on his face, which had for so many years disfigured him, had really been taken away without any pain to himself. He put up his hand to feel if any scar remained, but found that his right cheek was as smooth as his left.

The sun had long set, and the young moon had risen like a silver crescent in the sky. The old man suddenly realised how late it was and began to hurry home. He patted his right cheek all the time, as if to make sure of his good fortune in having lost the wen. He was so happy that he found it impossible to walk quietly – he ran and danced the whole way home.

He found his wife very anxious, wondering what had happened to make him so late. He soon told her all that had passed since he left home that afternoon. She was quite as happy as her husband when he showed her that the ugly lump had disappeared from his face, for in her youth she had prided herself on his good looks, and it had been a daily grief to her to see the horrid growth.

Now next door to this good old couple there lived a wicked and disagreeable old man. He, too, had for many years been troubled with the growth of a wen on his left cheek, and he, too, had tried all manner of things to get rid of it, but in vain.

He heard at once, through the servant, of his neighbour's

good luck in losing the lump on his face, so he called that very evening and asked his friend to tell him everything that concerned the loss of it. The good old man told his disagreeable neighbour all that had happened to him. He described the place where he would find the hollow tree in which to hide, and advised him to be on the spot in the late afternoon towards the time of sunset.

The old neighbour started out the very next afternoon, and after hunting about for some time, came to the hollow tree just as his friend had described. Here he hid himself and waited for the twilight.

Just as he had been told, the band of demons came at that hour and held a feast with dance and song. When this had gone on for some time, the chief of the demons looked around and said:

'It is now time for the old man to come as he promised us. Why doesn't he come?'

When the second old man heard these words he ran out of his hiding place in the tree and, kneeling down before the *Oni* (Demons), said:

'I have been waiting for a long time for you to speak!'

'Ah, you are the old man of yesterday,' said the demon chief. 'Thank you for coming, you must dance for us soon.'

The old man now stood up and opened his fan and began to dance. But he had never learned to dance, and knew nothing about the necessary gestures and different positions. He thought that anything would please the demons, so he just hopped about, waving his arms and stamping his feet, imitating as well as he could any dancing he had ever seen.

The *Oni* were very dissatisfied at this exhibition, and said amongst themselves:

'How badly he dances today!'

Then to the old man the demon chief said:

'Your performance today is quite different from the dance of yesterday. We don't wish to see any more of such dancing. We will give you back the pledge you left with us. You must go away at once.'

With these words he took out from a fold of his dress the lump which he had taken from the face of the old man who had danced so well the day before, and threw it at the right cheek of the old man who stood before him. The lump immediately attached itself to his cheek as firmly as if it had grown there always, and all attempts to pull it off were useless. The wicked old man, instead of losing the lump on his left cheek as he had hoped, found to his dismay that he had but added another to his right cheek in his attempt to get rid of the first.

He put up first one hand and then the other to each side of his face to make sure if he were not dreaming a horrible nightmare. No, sure enough there was now a great wen on the right side of his face as on the left. The demons had all disappeared, and there was nothing for him to do but to return home. He was a pitiful sight, for his face, with the two large lumps, one on each side, looked just like a Japanese gourd.

Y. T. O.
1903

The Story of Mimi-Nashi-Hōichi

More than 700 years ago, at Dan-no-ura in the Straits of Shi-monoséki, was fought the last battle of the long contest between the Heiké or Taira clan and the Genji or Minamoto clan. There the Heiké perished utterly, with their women and children, and their infant emperor likewise – now remembered as Antoku Tennō. And that sea and shore have been haunted for 700 years . . .

Elsewhere, I told you about the strange crabs found there, called Heiké crabs, which have human faces on their backs and are said to be the spirits of the Heiké warriors. But there are many strange things to be seen and heard along that coast. On dark nights, thousands of ghostly fires hover about the beach or flit above the waves – pale lights which the fishermen call *Oni-bi* or demon-fires; and, whenever the winds are up, a sound of great shouting comes from that sea like a clamour of battle.

In former years the Heiké were much more restless than they now are. They would rise about ships passing in the night and try to sink them; and at all times they would watch for swimmers, to pull them down. It was in order to appease those dead that the Buddhist temple Amidaji was built at Akamagaséki. A cemetery also was made close by, near the beach; and within it were set up monuments inscribed with the names of the drowned emperor and of his great vassals; and Buddhist services were regularly performed there, on behalf of the spirits of them. After the temple had been built and the tombs erected, the Heiké gave less trouble than before; but they continued to do queer things at intervals – proving that they had not found the perfect peace.

Some centuries ago there lived at Akamagaséki a blind man named Hōichi, who was famed for his skill in recitation and in playing upon the *biwa* (lute). From childhood he had been trained to recite and to play; and while yet a lad he had surpassed his teachers. As a professional *biwa-hōshi* (travelling performer or 'lute priest') he became famous chiefly by his recitations of the history of the Heiké and the Genji; and it is said that when he sang the song of the Battle of Dan-no-ura 'even the goblins (*kijin*) could not refrain from tears'.

At the outset of his career, Hōichi was very poor; but he found a good friend to help him. The priest of the Amidaji was fond of poetry and music; and he often invited Hōichi to the temple to play and recite. Afterwards, being much impressed by the wonderful skill of the lad, the priest proposed that Hōichi should make the temple his home; and this offer was gratefully accepted. Hōichi was given a room in the temple building; and, in return for food and lodging, he was required only to gratify the priest with a musical performance on certain evenings, when otherwise disengaged.

One summer night the priest was called away to perform a Buddhist service at the house of a dead parishioner; and he went there with his acolyte, leaving Hōichi alone in the temple. It was a hot night and the blind man sought to cool himself on the veranda before his sleeping-room. The veranda overlooked a small garden in the rear of the Amidaji. There Hōichi waited for the priest's return, and tried to relieve his solitude by practising upon his *biwa*. Midnight passed and the priest did not appear.

But the atmosphere was still too warm for comfort within doors and Hōichi remained outside. At last he heard steps approaching from the back gate. Somebody crossed the garden, advanced to the veranda, and halted directly in front of him – but it was not the priest. A deep voice called the blind man's name – abruptly and unceremoniously, in the manner of a samurai summoning an inferior:

'Hōichi!'

Hōichi was too much startled, for the moment, to respond; and the voice called again, in a tone of harsh command:

'Hōichi!'

'*Hai!* (Yes!)' answered the blind man, frightened by the menace in the voice. 'I am blind! – I cannot know who calls!'

'There is nothing to fear,' the stranger exclaimed, speaking more gently. 'I am stopping near this temple and have been sent to you with a message. My present lord, a person of exceedingly high rank, is now staying in Akamagaséki with many noble attendants. He wished to view the scene of the Battle of Dan-no-ura, and today he visited that place. Having heard of your skill in reciting the story of the battle, he now desires to hear your performance: so you will take your *biwa* and come with me at once to the house where the august assembly is waiting.'

In those times, the order of a samurai was not to be lightly disobeyed. Hōichi donned his sandals, took his *biwa* and went away with the stranger, who guided him deftly, but obliged him to walk very fast. The hand that guided was iron; and the clank of the warrior's stride proved him fully armed – probably some palace guard on duty. Hōichi's first alarm was over: he began to imagine himself in good luck; for, remembering the retainer's assurance about a 'person of exceedingly high rank', he thought that the lord who wished to hear the recitation could not be less than a daimio of the first class. Presently, the samurai halted and Hōichi became aware that they had arrived at a large gateway – and he wondered, for he could not remember any large gate in that part of the town, except the main gate of the Amidaji.

'*Kaimon!*'* the samurai called – and there was a sound of unbarring and the twain passed on. They traversed a space of garden and halted again before some entrance; and the retainer cried in a loud voice, 'Within there! I have brought Hōichi!' Then came sounds of feet hurrying and screens sliding, and rain-doors opening, and voices of women in converse. By the language of the women, Hōichi knew them to be domestics in some noble household; but he could not imagine to what place he had been conducted. Little time was allowed him for conjecture. After he had been helped to mount several stone steps, upon the last of which he was told to leave his sandals, a woman's hand guided him along interminable reaches of polished planking, and around pillared angles too many to remember, and over amazing widths of matted floor – into the middle of some vast apartment. There he thought that many great people were assembled: the sound of the rustling of silk was like the sound of leaves in a forest. He heard also a great humming of voices, talking in undertones; and the speech was the speech of courts.

Hōichi was told to put himself at ease, and he found a kneeling-cushion ready for him. After having taken his place upon it, and tuned his instrument, the voice of a woman – whom he divined to be the *rōjo* or matron in charge of the female service – addressed him, saying:

'It is now required that the history of the Heiké be recited, to the accompaniment of the *biwa*.'

* A respectful term, signifying the opening of a gate. It was used by samurai when calling to the guards on duty at a lord's gate for admission.

Now the entire recital would have required a time of many nights: therefore, Hōichi ventured a question:

'As the whole of the story is not soon told, what portion is it augustly desired that I now recite?'

The woman's voice made answer:

'Recite the story of the Battle at Dan-no-ura – for the pity of it is the most deep.'

Then Hōichi lifted up his voice and chanted the chant of the fight on the bitter sea, wonderfully making his *biwa* to sound like the straining of oars and the rushing of ships, the whirr and the hissing of arrows, the shouting and trampling of men, the crashing of steel upon helmets, the plunging of slain in the flood. And to left and right of him, in the pauses of his playing, he could hear voices murmuring praise:

'How marvellous an artist!'

'Never in our own province was playing heard like this!'

'Not in all the empire is there another singer like Hōichi!'

Then fresh courage came to him and he played and sang yet better than before; and a hush of wonder deepened about him. But when at last he came to tell the fate of the fair and helpless – the piteous perishing of the women and children – and the death-leap of Nii-no-Ama with the imperial infant in her arms – then all the listeners uttered together one long, long shuddering cry of anguish; and thereafter they wept and wailed so loudly and so wildly that the blind man was frightened by the violence and grief that he had made. For much time the sobbing and the wailing continued. But gradually the sounds of lamentation died away; and again, in the great stillness that followed, Hōichi heard the voice of the woman whom he supposed to be the *rōjo*. She said:

'Although we had been assured that you were a very skilful player upon the *biwa*, and without an equal in recitative, we did not know that anyone could be so skilful as you have proved

yourself tonight. Our lord has been pleased to say that he intends
to bestow upon you a fitting reward. But he desires that you
shall perform before him once every night for the next six
nights – after which time he will probably make his august
return journey. Tomorrow night, therefore, you are to come
here at the same hour. The retainer who tonight conducted you
will be sent for you . . . There is another matter about which I
have been ordered to inform you. It is required that you shall
speak to no one of your visits here, during the time of our lord's
august sojourn at Akamagaséki. As he is travelling incognito, he
commands that no mention of these things be made . . . You are
now free to go back to your temple.'

After Hōichi had duly expressed his thanks, a woman's hand
conducted him to the entrance of the house, where the same
retainer who had before guided him was waiting to take him
home. The retainer led him to the veranda at the rear of the
temple, and there bade him farewell.

It was almost dawn when Hōichi returned; but his absence
from the temple had not been observed – as the priest, coming
back at a very late hour, had supposed him asleep. During the
day Hōichi was able to take some rest; and he said nothing
about his strange adventure. In the middle of the following
night the samurai again came for him and led him to the august
assembly, where he gave another recitation with the same success that had attended his previous performance. But during
this second visit his absence from the temple was accidentally
discovered; and after his return in the morning he was summoned to the presence of the priest, who said to him, in a tone
of kindly reproach:

'We have been very anxious about you, friend Hōichi. To go
out, blind and alone, at so late an hour, is dangerous. Why did
you go without telling us? I could have ordered a servant to
accompany you. And where have you been?'

Hōichi answered, evasively:

'Pardon me, kind friend! I had to attend to some private business; and I could not arrange the matter at any other hour.'

The priest was surprised, rather than pained, by Hōichi's reticence: he felt it to be unnatural, and suspected something wrong. He feared that the blind lad had been bewitched or deluded by some evil spirits. He did not ask any more questions; but he privately instructed the menservants of the temple to keep watch upon Hōichi's movements, and to follow him in case he should again leave the temple after dark.

On the very next night, Hōichi was seen to leave the temple; and the servants immediately lighted their lanterns and followed after him. But it was a rainy night and very dark; and before the temple folks could get to the roadway, Hōichi had disappeared. Evidently, he had walked very fast — a strange thing, considering his blindness; for the road was in a bad condition. The men hurried through the streets, making inquiries at every house which Hōichi was accustomed to visit; but nobody could give them any news of him. At last, as they were returning to the temple by way of the shore, they were startled by the sound of a *biwa*, furiously played, in the cemetery of the Amidaji. Except for some ghostly fires — such as usually flitted there on dark nights — all was blackness in that direction. But the men at once hastened to the cemetery; and there, by the help of their lanterns, they discovered Hōichi — sitting alone in the rain before the memorial tomb of Antoku Tennō, making his *biwa* resound, and loudly chanting the chant of the Battle of Danno-ura. And behind him, and about him, and everywhere above the tombs, the fires of the dead were burning, like candles. Never before had so great a host of *Oni-bi* appeared in the sight of mortal man . . .

'Hōichi San! Hōichi San!' the servants cried. 'You are bewitched! Hōichi San!'

But the blind man did not seem to hear. Strenuously, he made his *biwa* to rattle and ring and clang; more and more wildly he chanted the chant of the Battle of Dan-no-ura. They caught hold of him; they shouted into his ear:

'Hōichi San! Hōichi San! Come home with us at once!'

Reprovingly, he spoke to them:

'To interrupt me in such a manner, before this august assembly, will not be tolerated.'

Whereat, in spite of the weirdness of the thing, the servants could not help laughing. Sure that he had been bewitched, they now seized him and pulled him up on his feet, and by main force hurried him back to the temple, where he was immediately relieved of his wet clothes by order of the priest. Then the priest insisted upon a full explanation of his friend's astonishing behaviour.

Hōichi long hesitated to speak. But at last, finding that his conduct had really alarmed and angered the good priest, he decided to abandon his reserve; and he related everything that had happened from the time of first visit of the samurai.

The priest said:

'Hōichi, my poor friend, you are now in great danger! How unfortunate that you did not tell me all this before! Your wonderful skill in music has indeed brought you into strange trouble. By this time you must be aware that you have not been visiting any house whatever, but have been passing your nights in the cemetery, among the tombs of the Heiké – and it was before the memorial tomb of Antoku Tennō that our people tonight found you, sitting in the rain. All that you have been imagining was illusion – except the calling of the dead. By once obeying them, you have put yourself in their power. If you obey them again, after what has already occurred, they will tear you in pieces. But they would have destroyed you, sooner or later, in any event . . . Now I shall not be able to remain with you tonight: I am called away to perform another service. But, before I go, it will be necessary to protect your body by writing holy texts upon it.'

Before sundown the priest and his acolyte stripped Hōichi: then, with their writing brushes, they traced upon his breast and back, head and face and neck, limbs and hands and feet – even upon the soles of his feet and upon all parts of his body – the text of the holy sutra called *Hannya-Shin-Kyō*. When this had been done, the priest instructed Hōichi, saying:

'Tonight, as soon as I go away, you must seat yourself on the veranda and wait. You will be called. But, whatever may happen, do not answer, and do not move. Say nothing and sit still – as if meditating. If you stir or make any noise, you will be torn asunder. Do not get frightened and do not think of calling for help – because no help could save you. If you do exactly as I tell you, the danger will pass and you will have nothing more to fear.'

After dark the priest and the acolyte went away; and Hōichi seated himself on the veranda, according to the instructions given him. He laid his *biwa* on the planking beside him, and, assuming the attitude of meditation, remained quite still, taking care not to cough or to breathe audibly. For hours he stayed thus.

Then, from the roadway, he heard the steps coming. They passed the gate, crossed the garden, approached the veranda, stopped – directly in front of him.

'Hōichi!' the deep voice called. But the blind man held his breath and sat motionless.

'Hōichi!' grimly called the voice a second time. Then a third time – savagely: 'Hōichi!'

Hōichi remained as still as a stone – and the voice grumbled:

'No answer! – that won't do! . . . Must see where the fellow is.'

There was a noise of heavy feet mounting upon the veranda.

The feet approached deliberately, halted beside him. Then, for long minutes – during which Hōichi felt his whole body shake to the beating of his heart – there was dead silence.

At last the gruff voice muttered close to him:

'Here is the *biwa*, but of the *biwa*-player I see – only two ears! . . . So that explains why he did not answer: he had no mouth to answer with – there is nothing left of him but his ears . . . Now to my lord those ears I will take – in proof that the august commands have been obeyed, so far as was possible.'

At that instant Hōichi felt his ears gripped by fingers of iron – and torn off! Great as the pain was, he gave no cry. The heavy footfalls receded along the veranda, descended into the garden, passed out to the roadway – ceased. From either side of his head, the blind man felt a thick warm trickling; but he dared not lift his hands . . .

Before sunrise the priest came back. He hastened at once to the veranda in the rear, stepped and slipped upon something clammy, and uttered a cry of horror – for he saw, by the light of his lantern, that the clamminess was blood. But he perceived Hōichi sitting there in the attitude of meditation – with the blood still oozing from his wounds.

'My poor Hōichi!' cried the startled priest. 'What is this? . . . You have been hurt?'

At the sound of his friend's voice, the blind man felt safe. He burst out sobbing, and tearfully told his adventure of the night.

'Poor, poor Hōichi!' the priest exclaimed. 'All my fault! My very grievous fault! . . . Everywhere upon your body the holy texts had been written – except upon your ears! I trusted my acolyte to do that part of the work; and it was very, very wrong of me not to have made sure that he had done it! . . . Well, the matter cannot now be helped; we can only try to heal your hurts as soon as possible . . . Cheer up, friend! – the danger is now well over. You will never again be troubled by those visitors.'

With the aid of a good doctor, Hōichi soon recovered from his injuries. The story of his strange adventure spread far and wide, and soon made him famous. Many noble persons went to Akamagaséki to hear him recite; and large presents of money were given to him – so that he became a wealthy man . . . But from the time of his adventure, he was known only by the appellation of Mimi-Nashi-Hōichi: 'Hōichi-the-Earless'.

L. H.

1904

Fragment

And it was at the hour of sunset that they came to the foot of the mountain. There was in that place no sign of life – neither token of water, nor trace of plant, nor shadow of flying bird – nothing but desolation rising to desolation. And the summit was lost in heaven.

Then the Bodhisattva said to his young companion:

'What you have asked to see will be shown to you. But the place of the Vision is far; and the way is rude. Follow after me, and do not fear: strength will be given you.'

Twilight gloomed about them as they climbed. There was no beaten path, nor any mark of former human visitation; and the way was over an endless heaping of tumbled fragments that rolled or turned beneath the foot. Sometimes a mass dislodged would clatter down with hollow echoings; sometimes the substance trodden would burst like an empty shell . . . Stars pointed and thrilled; and the darkness deepened.

'Do not fear, my son,' said the Bodhisattva, guiding. 'Danger there is none, though the way be grim.'

Under the stars they climbed – fast, fast – mounting by help of power superhuman. High zones of mist they passed; and they saw below them, ever widening as they climbed, a soundless flood of cloud, like the tide of a milky sea.

Hour after hour they climbed; and forms invisible yielded to their tread with dull, soft crashings; and faint, cold fires lighted and died at every breaking.

And once the pilgrim youth laid hand on a something smooth that was not stone – and lifted it – and dimly saw the cheekless gibe of death.

'Linger not thus, my son!' urged the voice of the teacher. 'The summit that we must gain is very far away!'

On through the dark they climbed – and felt continually beneath them the soft, strange breakings – and saw the icy fires worm and die – till the rim of the night turned grey and the stars began to fail, and the east began to bloom.

Yet still they climbed – fast, fast – mounting by help of power superhuman. About them now was frigidness of death – and silence tremendous . . . A gold flame kindled in the east.

Then first to the pilgrim's gaze the steeps revealed their nakedness – and a trembling seized him, and a ghastly fear. For there was not any ground – neither beneath him nor about him nor above him – but a heaping only, monstrous and measureless, of skulls and fragments of skulls and dust of bone – with a shimmer of shed teeth strewn through the drift of it, like the shimmer of scrags of shell in the wrack of a tide.

'Do not fear, my son!' cried the voice of the Bodhisattva. 'Only the strong of heart can win to the place of the Vision!'

Behind them the world had vanished. Nothing remained but the clouds beneath and the sky above, and the heaping of skulls between, up-slanting out of sight.

Then the sun climbed with the climbers; and there was no warmth in the light of him, but coldness sharp as a sword. And the horror of stupendous height, and the nightmare of stupendous depth, and the terror of silence, ever grew and grew, and weighed upon the pilgrim, and held his feet – so that suddenly all power departed from him and he moaned like a sleeper in dreams.

'Hasten, hasten, my son!' cried the Bodhisattva. 'The day is brief and the summit is very far away.'

But the pilgrim shrieked:

'I fear! I fear unspeakably! – and the power has departed from me!'

'The power will return, my son,' made answer the Bodhisattva. 'Look now below you and above you and about you, and tell me what you see.'

'I cannot,' cried the pilgrim, trembling and clinging. 'I dare not look beneath! Before me and about me there is nothing but skulls of men.'

'And yet, my son,' said the Bodhisattva, laughing softly, 'and yet you do not know of what this mountain is made.'

The other, shuddering, repeated:

'I fear! – unutterably, I fear! . . . There is nothing but skulls of men!'

'A mountain of skulls it is,' responded the Bodhisattva. 'But know, my son, that all of them ARE YOUR OWN! Each has at some time been the nest of your dreams and delusions and desires. Not even one of them is the skull of any other being. All – all without exception – have been yours, in the billions of your former lives.'

L. H.
1899

Furisodé

Recently, while passing through a little street tenanted chiefly by dealers in old wares, I noticed a *furisodé* or long-sleeved robe of the rich purple tint called *murasaki*, hanging before one of the shops. It was a robe such as might have been worn by a lady of rank in the time of the Tokugawa. I stopped to look at the five crests upon it; and in the same moment there came to my recollection this legend of a similar robe said to have once caused the destruction of Tokyo.

Nearly 250 years ago, the daughter of a rich merchant of the city of the Shoguns, while attending some temple festival, perceived in the crowd a young samurai of remarkable beauty and immediately fell in love with him. Unhappily for her, he disappeared in the press before she could learn through her attendants who he was or whence he had come. But his image remained vivid in her memory, even to the least detail of his costume. The holiday attire then worn by samurai youths was scarcely less brilliant than that of young girls; and the upper dress of this handsome stranger had seemed wonderfully beautiful to the enamoured maiden. She fancied that by wearing a robe of like quality and colour, bearing the same crest, she might be able to attract his notice on some future occasion.

Accordingly, she had such a robe made, with very long

sleeves, according to the fashion of the period; and she prized it greatly. She wore it whenever she went out; and when at home she would suspend it in her room, and try to imagine the form of her unknown beloved within it. Sometimes she would pass hours before it, dreaming and weeping by turns. And she would pray to the gods and the Buddhas that she might win the young man's affection, often repeating the invocation of the Nichiren sect: *Namu Myōhō Renge Kyō!*

But she never saw the youth again; and she pined with longing for him, and sickened, and died and was buried. After her burial, the long-sleeved robe that she had so much prized was given to the Buddhist temple of which her family were parishioners. It is an old custom to thus dispose of the garments of the dead.

The priest was able to sell the robe at a good price; for it was a costly silk and bore no trace of the tears that had fallen upon it. It was bought by a girl of about the same age as the dead lady. She wore it only one day. Then she fell sick and began to act strangely — crying out that she was haunted by the vision of a beautiful young man, and that for love of him she was going to die. And within a little while she died; and the long-sleeved robe was a second time presented to the temple.

Again the priest sold it; and again it became the property of a young girl, who wore it only once. Then she also sickened and talked of a beautiful shadow, and died and was buried. And the robe was given a third time to the temple; and the priest wondered and doubted.

Nevertheless, he ventured to sell the luckless garment once more. Once more it was purchased by a girl and once more worn; and the wearer pined and died. And the robe was given a fourth time to the temple.

Then the priest felt sure that there was some evil influence at work; and he told his acolytes to make a fire in the temple court and to burn the robe.

So they made a fire, into which the robe was thrown. But as the silk began to burn, there suddenly appeared upon it dazzling characters of flame – the characters of the invocation *Namu Myōhō Renge Kyō* – and these, one by one, leaped like great sparks to the temple roof; and the temple took fire.

Embers from the burning temple presently dropped upon neighbouring roofs; and the whole street was soon ablaze. Then a sea wind, rising, blew destruction into further streets; and the conflagration spread from street to street, and from district into district, till nearly the whole of the city was consumed. And this calamity, which occurred upon the eighteenth day of the first month of the first year of Meiréki (1655), is still remembered in Tokyo as the *Furisodé-Kwaji* – the Great Fire of the Long-sleeved Robe.

According to a storybook called *Kibun-Daijin*, the name of the girl who caused the robe to be made was O-Samé; and she was the daughter of Hikoyemon, a wine merchant of Hyakushō-machi in the district of Azabu. Because of her beauty she was also called Azabu-Komachi or the Komachi of Azabu.* The same book says that the temple of the tradition was a Nichiren temple called Hon-myoji in the district of Hongō; and that the crest upon the robe was a *kikyō* flower. But there are many different versions of the story; and I distrust the *Kibun-Daijin* because it asserts that the beautiful samurai was not really a man, but a transformed dragon or water serpent that used to inhabit the lake at Ueno, Shinobazu no Ike.

L. H.
1899

---

* Ono-no-Komachi (*c.* 825–*c.* 900) was the most beautiful woman of her time, and so great a poet that she could move heaven by her verses and cause rain to fall in time of drought.

The Kakemono Ghost of Aki Province

Down the Inland Sea, between Umedaichi and Kure (now a great naval port) and in the Province of Aki, there is a small village called Yaiyama, in which lived a painter of some note, Abe Tenko. Abe Tenko taught more than he painted, and relied for his living mostly on the small means to which he had succeeded at his father's death, and on the aspiring artists who boarded in the village for the purpose of taking daily lessons from him. The island and rock scenery in the neighbourhood afforded continual study, and Tenko was never short of pupils. Among them was one scarcely more than a boy, being only seventeen years of age. His name was Sawara Kameju, and a most promising pupil he was. He had been sent to Tenko over a year before, when scarce sixteen years of age, and, for the reason that Tenko had been a friend of his father, Sawara was taken under the roof of the artist and treated as if he had been his son.

Tenko had had a sister who went into the service of the Lord of Aki, by whom she had a daughter. Had the child been a son, it would have been adopted into the Aki family; but being a daughter, it was, according to Japanese custom, sent back to its mother's family, with the result that Tenko took charge of the child, whose name was Kimi. The mother being dead, the child had lived with him for sixteen years. Our story opens with O Kimi grown into a pretty girl.

O Kimi was a most devoted adopted daughter to Tenko. She attended almost entirely to his household affairs, and Tenko looked upon her as if indeed she were his own daughter, instead of an illegitimate niece, trusting her in everything.

After the arrival of the young student, O Kimi's heart gave her much trouble. She fell in love with him. Sawara admired O Kimi greatly; but of love he never said a word, being too much absorbed in his study. He looked upon Kimi as a sweet girl, taking his meals with her and enjoying her society. He would have fought for her and he loved her, but he never gave himself time to think that she was not his sister, and that he might make love to her. So it came to pass at last that O Kimi one day, with the pains of love in her heart, availed herself of her guardian's absence at the temple, whither he had gone to paint something for the priests. O Kimi screwed up her courage and made love to Sawara. She told him that since he had come to the house her heart had known no peace. She loved him and would like to marry him if he did not mind.

This simple and maidenlike request, accompanied by the offer of tea, was more than young Sawara was able to answer without acquiescence. After all, it did not much matter, thought he: 'Kimi is a most beautiful and charming girl, and I like her very much, and must marry some day.'

So Sawara told Kimi that he loved her and would be only too delighted to marry her when his studies were complete – say, two or three years thence. Kimi was overjoyed, and on the return of the good Tenko from Korinji Temple informed her guardian of what had passed.

Sawara set to with renewed vigour and worked diligently, improving very much in his style of painting; and after a year Tenko thought it would do him good to finish off his studies in

Kyoto under an old friend of his own, a painter named Sumi-yoshi Myokei. Thus it was that in the spring of the sixth year of Kioho – that is, in 1721 – Sawara bade farewell to Tenko and his pretty niece O Kimi, and started forth to the capital. It was a sad parting. Sawara had grown to love Kimi very deeply, and he vowed that as soon as his name was made he would return and marry her.

In the olden days the Japanese were even more shockingly poor correspondents than they are now, and even lovers or engaged couples did not write to each other, as several of my tales may show.

After Sawara had been away for a year, it seemed that he should write and say at all events how he was getting on; but he did not do so. A second year passed, and still there was no news. In the meantime, there had been several admirers of O Kimi's who had proposed to Tenko for her hand; but Tenko had invari-ably said that Kimi San was already engaged – until one day he heard from Myokei, the painter in Kyoto, who told him that Sawara was making splendid progress, and that he was most anxious that the youth should marry his daughter. He felt that he must ask his old friend Tenko first, and before speaking to Sawara.

Tenko, on the other hand, had an application from a rich merchant for O Kimi's hand. What was Tenko to do? Sawara showed no signs of returning; on the contrary, it seemed that Myokei was anxious to get him to marry into his family.

'That must be a good thing for Sawara,' he thought. 'Myokei is a better teacher than I, and if Sawara marries his daughter he will take more interest than ever in my old pupil. Also, it is advis-able that Kimi should marry that rich young merchant, if I can persuade her to do so; but it will be difficult, for she loves Sawara still. I am afraid he has forgotten her. A little strategy I will try, and tell her that Myokei has written to tell me that Sawara is going to marry his daughter; then, possibly, she may feel sufficiently vengeful to agree to marry the young merchant.'

Arguing thus to himself, he wrote to Myokei to say that he had his full consent to ask Sawara to be his son-in-law, and he wished him every success in the effort; and in the evening he spoke to Kimi.

'Kimi,' he said, 'today I have had news of Sawara through my friend Myokei.'

'Oh, do tell me what!' cried the excited Kimi. 'Is he coming back, and has he finished his education? How delighted I shall be to see him! We can be married in April, when the cherry blooms, and he can paint a picture of our first picnic.'

'I fear, Kimi, the news which I have does not talk of his coming back. On the contrary, I am asked by Myokei to allow Sawara to marry his daughter, and, as I think such a request could not have been made had Sawara been faithful to you, I have answered that I have no objection to the union. And now, as for yourself, I deeply regret to tell you this; but as your uncle and guardian I again wish to impress upon you the advisability of marrying Yorozuya, the young merchant, who is deeply in love with you and in every way a most desirable husband; indeed, I must insist upon it, for I think it most desirable.'

Poor O Kimi San broke into tears and deep sobs, and without answering a word went to her room, where Tenko thought it well to leave her alone for the night.

In the morning she had gone, none knew whither, there being no trace of her.

Up in Kyoto, Sawara continued his studies, true and faithful to O Kimi. After receiving Tenko's letter approving of Myokei's asking Sawara to become his son-in-law, Myokei asked Sawara if he would so honour him:

'When you marry my daughter, we shall be a family of

painters, and I think you will be one of the most celebrated ones that Japan ever had.'

'But, sir,' cried Sawara, 'I cannot do myself the honour of marrying your daughter, for I am already engaged – I have been for the last three years – to Kimi, Tenko's daughter. It is most strange that he should not have told you!'

There was nothing for Myokei to say to this; but there was much for Sawara to think about. Foolish, perhaps he then thought, were the ways of Japanese in not corresponding more freely. He wrote to Kimi twice, accordingly, but no answer came. Then Myokei fell ill of a chill and died: so Sawara returned to his village home in Aki, where he was welcomed by Tenko, who was now, without O Kimi, lonely in his old age.

When Sawara heard that Kimi had gone away, leaving neither address nor letter, he was very angry, for he had not been told the reason.

'An ungrateful and bad girl,' said he to Tenko, 'and I have been lucky indeed in not marrying her!'

'Yes, yes,' said Tenko, 'you have been lucky, but you must not be too angry. Women are queer things, and, as the saying goes, when you see water running uphill and hens laying square eggs you may expect to see a truly honest-minded woman. But come now – I want to tell you that, as I am growing old and feeble, I wish to make you the master of my house and property here. You must take my name and marry!'

Feeling disgusted at O Kimi's conduct, Sawara readily consented. A pretty young girl, the daughter of a wealthy farmer, was found – Kiku (Chrysanthemum) – and she and Sawara lived happily with old Tenko, keeping his house and minding his estate. Sawara painted in his spare time. Little by little, he became quite famous. One day the Lord of Aki sent for him and said it was his wish that Sawara should paint the seven beautiful scenes of the Islands of Kabakarijima; the pictures were to be mounted on gold screens.

This was the first commission that Sawara had had from such a high official. He was very proud of it, and went off to the Upper and Lower Kabakari Islands, where he made rough sketches. He went also to the rocky islands of Shokokujima, and to the little uninhabited island of Daikokujima, where an adventure befell him.

Strolling along the shore, he met a girl, tanned by sun and wind. She wore only a red cotton cloth about her loins, and her hair fell upon her shoulders. She had been gathering shellfish, and had a basket of them under her arm. Sawara thought it strange that he should meet a single woman in so wild a place, and more so still when she addressed him, saying, 'Surely you are Sawara Kameju – are you not?'

'Yes,' answered Sawara, 'I am, but it is very strange that you should know me. May I ask how you do so?'

'If you are Sawara, as I know you are, you should know me without asking, for I am no other than Kimi, to whom you were engaged!'

Sawara was astonished, and hardly knew what to say: so he asked her questions as to how she had come to this lonely island. O Kimi explained everything and ended by saying, with a smile of happiness upon her face:

'And since, my dearest Sawara, I understand that what I was told is false, and that you did not marry Myokei's daughter, and that we have been faithful to each other, we can be married and happy after all. Oh, think how happy we shall be!'

'Alas, alas, my dearest Kimi, it cannot be! I was led to suppose that you had deserted our benefactor Tenko and given up all thought of me. Oh, the sadness of it all, the wickedness! I have been persuaded that you were faithless, and have been made to marry another!'

O Kimi made no answer, but began to run along the shore towards a little hut, which home she had made for herself. She ran fast and Sawara ran after her, calling, 'Kimi! Kimi! Stop and speak to me!' – but Kimi did not stop. She gained her hut, and, seizing a knife, plunged it into her throat and fell back, bleeding to death. Sawara, greatly grieved, burst into tears. It was horrible to see the girl who might have been his bride lying dead at his feet all covered with blood, and having suffered so horrible a death at her own hands. Greatly impressed, he drew paper from his pocket and made a sketch of the body. Then he and his boatman buried O Kimi above the tidemark near the primitive hut. Afterwards, at home, with a mournful heart, he painted a picture of the dead girl and hung it in his room.

On the first night that it was hung, Sawara had a dreadful dream. On awakening he found the figure on the kakemono* seemed to be alive: the ghost of O Kimi stepped out of it and stood near his bed. Night after night the ghost appeared, until sleep and rest for Sawara were no longer possible. There was nothing to be done, thought he, but to send his wife back to her parents, which he did; and the kakemono he presented to the Korinji Temple, where the priests kept it with great care and daily prayed for the spirit of O Kimi San. After that, Sawara saw the ghost no more.

R. G. S.
1908

---

* A Japanese painting on paper or silk, displayed as a wall hanging.

A Dead Secret

A long time ago, in the Province of Tamba, there lived a rich merchant named Inamuraya Gensuké. He had a daughter called O-Sono. As she was very clever and pretty, he thought it would be a pity to let her grow up with only such teaching as the country teachers could give her: so he sent her, in care of some trusty attendants, to Kyoto, that she might be trained in the polite accomplishments taught to the ladies of the capital. After she had thus been educated, she was married to a friend of her father's family – a merchant named Nagaraya – and she lived happily with him for nearly four years. They had one child, a boy. But O-Sono fell ill and died in the fourth year after her marriage.

On the night after the funeral of O-Sono, her little son said that his mamma had come back and was in the room upstairs. She had smiled at him, but would not talk to him: so he became afraid and ran away. Then some of the family went upstairs to the room which had been O-Sono's; and they were startled to see, by the light of a small lamp which had been kindled before a shrine in that room, the figure of the dead mother. She appeared as if standing in front of a *tansu* or chest of drawers, that still contained her ornaments and her wearing apparel. Her head and shoulders could be very distinctly seen; but from the waist downwards the figure thinned into invisibility – it was like an imperfect reflection of her, and transparent as a shadow on water.

Then the folk were afraid and left the room. Below, they consulted together; and the mother of O-Sono's husband said:

'A woman is fond of her small things, and O-Sono was much attached to her belongings. Perhaps she has come back to look at them. Many dead persons will do that – unless the things be given to the parish temple. If we present O-Sono's robes and girdles to the temple, her spirit will probably find rest.'

It was agreed that this should be done as soon as possible. So, on the following morning, the drawers were emptied and all of O-Sono's ornaments and dresses were taken to the temple. But she came back the next night and looked at the *tansu* as before. And she came back also on the night following, and the night after that, and every night – and the house became a house of fear.

The mother of O-Sono's husband then went to the parish temple and told the chief priest all that had happened, and asked for ghostly counsel. The temple was a Zen temple and the head priest was a learned old man, known as Daigen Oshō. He said:

'There must be something about which she is anxious, in or near that *tansu*.'

'But we emptied all the drawers,' replied the woman. 'There is nothing in the *tansu*.'

'Well,' said Daigen Oshō, 'tonight I shall go to your house and keep watch in that room, and see what can be done. You must give orders that no person shall enter the room while I am watching, unless I call.'

After sundown, Daigen Oshō went to the house and found the room made ready for him. He remained there alone, reading the sutras; and nothing appeared until after the Hour of the Rat (11 p.m. to 1 a.m.). Then the figure of O-Sono suddenly outlined itself in front of the *tansu*. Her face had a wistful look and she kept her eyes fixed upon the *tansu*.

The priest uttered the holy formula prescribed in such cases, and then, addressing the figure by the *kaimyō*★ of O-Sono, said:

'I have come here in order to help you. Perhaps in that *tansu* there is something about which you have reason to feel anxious. Shall I try to find it for you?'

The shadow appeared to give assent by a slight motion of the head; and the priest, rising, opened the top drawer. It was empty. Successively, he opened the second, the third and the fourth drawer; he searched carefully, behind them and beneath them; he carefully examined the interior of the chest. He found nothing. But the figure remained gazing as wistfully as before.

'What can she want?' thought the priest.

Suddenly, it occurred to him that there might be something hidden under the paper with which the drawers were lined. He removed the lining of the first drawer – nothing! He removed the lining of the second and third drawers – still nothing. But under the lining of the lowermost drawer he found – a letter.

'Is this the thing about which you have been troubled?' he asked.

The shadow of the woman turned towards him, her faint gaze fixed upon the letter.

'Shall I burn it for you?' he asked.

She bowed before him.

'It shall be burned in the temple this very morning,' he promised, 'and no one shall read it, except myself.'

The figure smiled and vanished.

Dawn was breaking as the priest descended the stairs to find the family waiting anxiously below.

★ The posthumous Buddhist name, or religious name, given to the dead.

'Do not be anxious,' he said to them. 'She will not appear again.'

And she never did.

The letter was burned. It was a love letter written to O-Sono in the time of her studies at Kyoto. But the priest alone knew what was in it, and the secret died with him.

L. H.

1904

The Nun of the Temple of Amida

I

When O-Toyo's husband – a distant cousin, adopted into her family for love's sake – had been summoned by his lord to the capital, she did not feel anxious about the future. She felt sad only. It was the first time since their bridal that they had ever been separated. But she had her father and mother to keep her company, and, dearer than either – though she would never have confessed it even to herself – her little son. Besides, she always had plenty to do. There were many household duties to perform, and there was much clothing to be woven – both silk and cotton.

Once daily, at a fixed hour, she would set for the absent husband, in his favourite room, little repasts faultlessly served on dainty lacquered trays – miniature meals such as are offered to the ghosts of the ancestors and to the gods.* These repasts were served at the east side of the room, and his kneeling-cushion placed before them. The reason they were served at the east side was because he had gone east. Before removing the food, she

* Such a repast, offered to the spirit of the absent loved one, is called a *Kagé-zen* (literally, 'Shadow-tray'). The word '*zen*' is also used to signify the meal served on the lacquered tray, which has feet like a miniature table. So that the term 'Shadow-feast' would be a better translation of *Kagé-zen*.

always lifted the cover of the little soup bowl to see if there was vapour upon its lacquered inside surface. For it is said that if there be vapour on the inside of the lid covering food so offered, the absent beloved is well. But if there be none, he is dead – because that is a sign that his soul has returned by itself to seek nourishment. O-Toyo found the lacquer thickly beaded with vapour day by day.

The child was her constant delight. He was three years old and fond of asking questions to which none but the gods knew the real answers. When he wanted to play, she laid aside her work to play with him. When he wanted to rest, she told him wonderful stories or gave pretty, pious answers to his questions about those things which no man can ever understand. At evening, when the little lamps had been lighted before the holy tablets and the images, she taught his lips to shape the words of filial prayer. When he had been laid to sleep, she brought her work near him and watched the still sweetness of his face. Sometimes he would smile in his dreams; and she knew that Kwannon the divine★ was playing shadowy play with him, and she would murmur the Buddhist invocation to that Maid, 'who looketh forever down above the sound of prayer'.

Sometimes, in the season of very clear days, she would climb the mountain of Dakeyama, carrying her little boy on her back. Such a trip delighted him much, not only because of what his mother taught him to see, but also of what she taught him to hear. The sloping way was through groves and woods, and over grassed slopes and around queer rocks; and there were flowers with stories in their hearts, and trees holding tree spirits. Pigeons cried *korup-korup*, and doves sobbed *owaō, owaō*, and cicadas wheezed and fluted and tinkled.

All those who wait for absent dear ones make – if they can – a

★ The goddess of compassion and mercy.

pilgrimage to the peak called Dakeyama. It is visible from any part of the city; and from its summit several provinces can be seen. At the very top is a stone of almost human height and shape, perpendicularly set up; and little pebbles are heaped before it and upon it. And nearby there is a small Shintō shrine erected to the spirit of a princess of other days. For she mourned the absence of one she loved, and used to watch from this mountain for his coming, until she pined away and was changed into a stone. The people, therefore, built the shrine; and lovers of the absent still pray there for the return of those dear to them; and each, after so praying, takes home one of the little pebbles heaped there. And when the beloved one returns, the pebble must be taken back to the pebble pile upon the mountaintop, and other pebbles with it, for a thank-offering and commemoration.

Always, ere O-Toyo and her son could reach their home after such a day, the dusk would fall softly about them; for the way was long, and they had to both go and return by boat through the wilderness of rice fields around the town – which is a slow manner of journeying. Sometimes stars and fireflies lighted them; sometimes also the moon – and O-Toyo would softly sing to her boy the Izumo child-song to the moon:

> Nono San,
> Little Lady Moon,
> How old are you?
> 'Thirteen days –
> Thirteen and nine.'
> That is still young,
> And the reason must be
> For that bright red obi,*
> So nicely tied,

* A broad sash worn around the waist of a kimono. A very brightly coloured obi can be worn only by children.

> And that nice white girdle
> About your hips.
> Will you give it to the horse?
> 'Oh, no, no!'
> Will you give it to the cow?
> 'Oh, no, no!'

And up to the blue night would rise from all those wet leagues of laboured field that great soft bubbling chorus, which seems the very voice of the soil itself – the chant of the frogs. And O-Toyo would interpret its syllables to the child: *Mé kayui! Mé kayui!* 'Mine eyes tickle; I want to sleep.'

All those were happy hours.

II

Then, twice, within the time of three days, those masters of life and death whose ways belong to the eternal mysteries struck at her heart. First she was taught that the gentle husband for whom she had so often prayed never could return to her – having been returned unto that dust out of which all forms are borrowed. And in another little while she knew her boy slept so deep a sleep that the Chinese physician could not waken him. These things she learned only as shapes are learned in lightning flashes. Between and beyond the flashes was that absolute darkness which is the pity of the gods.

It passed; and she rose to meet a foe whose name is Memory. Before all others she could keep her face, as in other days, sweet and smiling. But when alone with this visitant, she found herself less strong. She would arrange little toys and spread out little dresses on the matting, and look at them, and talk to them in whispers, and smile silently. But the smile would ever end in a burst of wild, loud weeping; and she would beat her head upon the floor, and ask foolish questions of the gods.

One day she thought of a weird consolation – that rite the people name '*Toritsu-banashi*' – the evocation of the dead. Could she not call back her boy for one brief minute only? It would trouble the little soul; but would he not gladly bear a moment's pain for her dear sake? Surely!

(To have the dead called back one must go to some priest – Buddhist or Shintō – who knows the rite of incantation. And the mortuary tablet or *ihai* of the dead must be brought to that priest. Then ceremonies of purification are performed; candles are lighted and incense is kindled before the *ihai*; and prayers or parts of sutras are recited; and offerings of flowers and of rice are made. But in this case, the rice must not be cooked. And when everything has been made ready, the priest – taking in his left hand an instrument shaped like a bow and striking it rapidly with his right – calls upon the name of the dead, and cries out the words, '*Kitazo yo! Kitazo yo! Kitazo yo!*', meaning, 'I have come!' And, as he cries, the tone of his voice gradually changes until it becomes the very voice of the dead person – for the ghost enters into him. Then the dead will answer questions quickly asked, but will cry continually, 'Hasten, hasten! For this my coming back is painful, and I have but a little time to stay!' And, having answered, the ghost passes; and the priest falls senseless upon his face. Now to call back the dead is not good. For by calling them back their condition is made worse. Returning to the underworld, they must take a place lower than that which they held before. Today these rites are not allowed by law. They once consoled, but the law is a good law and just – since there exist men willing to mock the divine which is in human hearts.)

So it came to pass that O-Toyo found herself one night in a lonely little temple at the verge of the city – kneeling before the *ihai* of her boy and hearing the rite of incantation. And, presently, out of the lips of the officiant, there came a voice she thought she knew, a voice loved above all others – but faint and very thin, like a sobbing of wind.

And the thin voice cried to her:

'Ask quickly, quickly, Mother! Dark is the way and long, and I may not linger.'

Then, tremblingly, she questioned:

'Why must I sorrow for my child? What is the justice of the gods?'

And there was answer given:

'O Mother, do not mourn me thus! That I died was only that you might not die. For the year was a year of sickness and of sorrow – and it was given me to know that you were to die, and I obtained by prayer that I should take your place.

'O Mother, never weep for me! It is not kindness to mourn for the dead. Over the River of Tears their silent road is; and when mothers weep, the flood of that river rises and the soul cannot pass, but must wander to and fro.

'Therefore, I pray you, do not grieve, O mother mine! Only give me a little water sometimes.'

III

From that hour she was not seen to weep. She performed, lightly and silently, as in former days, the gentle duties of a daughter.

Seasons passed, and her father thought to find another husband for her. To the mother, he said:

'If our daughter again have a son, it will be great joy for her, and for all of us.'

But the wiser mother made answer:

'Unhappy she is not. It is impossible that she marry again. She has become as a little child, knowing nothing of trouble or sin.'

It was true that she had ceased to know real pain. She had begun to show a strange fondness for very small things. At first she had found her bed too large – perhaps through the sense of emptiness left by the loss of her child; then, day by day, other things seemed to grow too large – the dwelling itself, the familiar rooms, the alcove and its great flower vases – even the household utensils. She wished to eat her rice with miniature chopsticks out of a very small bowl such as children use.

In these things she was lovingly humoured; and in other matters she was not fantastic. The old people consulted together about her constantly. At last the father said:

'For our daughter to live with strangers might be painful. But as we are aged, we may soon have to leave her. Perhaps we could provide for her by making her a nun. We might build a little temple for her.'

Next day the mother asked O-Toyo:

'Would you not like to become a holy nun and to live in a very, very small temple, with a very small altar, and little images of the Buddhas? We should be always near you. If you wish this, we shall get a priest to teach you the sutras.'

O-Toyo wished it, and asked that an extremely small nun's dress be got for her. But the mother said:

'Everything except the dress a good nun may have made small. But she must wear a large dress – that is the law of Buddha.'

So she was persuaded to wear the same dress as other nuns.

IV

They built for her a small *An-dera* or Nun's Temple, in an empty court where another and larger temple, called Amidaji, had once stood. The *An-dera* was also called Amidaji, and was dedicated to Amida-Nyōrai and to other Buddhas. It was fitted up with a very small altar and with miniature altar furniture. There was a tiny copy of the sutras on a tiny reading desk, and tiny screens and bells and kakemono. And she dwelt there long after her parents had passed away. People called her the Amidaji no Bikuni, which means The Nun of the Temple of Amida.

A little outside the gate there was a statue of Jizo. This Jizo was a special Jizo – the friend of sick children. There were nearly always offerings of small rice cakes to be seen before him. These signified that some sick child was being prayed for; and the number of the rice cakes signified the number of the years of the child. Most often there were but two or three cakes; rarely there were seven or ten. The Amidaji no Bikuni took care of the statue, and supplied it with incense offerings and flowers from the temple garden; for there was a small garden behind the An-dera.

After making her morning round with her alms bowl, she would usually seat herself before a very small loom, to weave cloth much too narrow for serious use. But her webs were bought always by certain shopkeepers who knew her story; and they made her presents of very small cups, tiny flower vases and queer dwarf trees for her garden.

Her greatest pleasure was the companionship of children; and this she never lacked. Japanese child-life is mostly passed in temple courts; and many happy childhoods were spent in the court of the Amidaji. All the mothers in that street liked to have their little ones play there, but cautioned them never to laugh at the Bikuni San.

'Sometimes her ways are strange,' they would say, 'but that is because she once had a little son who died, and the pain became too great for her mother's heart. So you must be very good and respectful to her.'

Good they were, but not quite respectful in the reverential sense. They knew better than to be that. They called her 'Bikuni San' always and saluted her nicely, but otherwise they treated her like one of themselves. They played games with her; and she gave them tea in extremely small cups, and made for them heaps of rice cakes not much bigger than peas, and wove upon her loom cloth of cotton and cloth of silk for the robes of their dolls. So she became to them as a blood-sister.

They played with her daily till they grew too big to play, and left the court of the temple of Amida to begin the bitter work of life, and to become the fathers and mothers of children whom they sent to play in their stead. These learned to love the Bikuni San like their parents had done. And the Bikuni San lived to play with the children of the children of the children of those who remembered when her temple was built.

The people took good heed that she should not know want. There was always given to her more than she needed for herself. So she was able to be nearly as kind to the children as she wished, and to feed extravagantly certain small animals. Birds nested in her temple and ate from her hand, and learned not to perch upon the heads of the Buddhas.

Some days after her funeral, a crowd of children visited my house. A little girl of nine years spoke for them all:

'Sir, we are asking for the sake of the Bikuni San who is dead. A very large *haka* (tombstone) has been set up for her. It is a nice *haka*. But we want to give her also a very, very small *haka*, because in the time she was with us she often said that she would like a very little *haka*. And the stone-cutter has promised to cut it for us, and to make it very pretty, if we can bring the money. Therefore, perhaps you will honourably give something.'

'Assuredly,' I said. 'But now you will have nowhere to play.'

She answered, smiling:

'We shall still play in the court of the temple of Amida. She is buried there. She will hear our playing, and be glad.'

L. H.
1923

Discover more in **VINTAGE CLASSICS** red spine